PAWN

L. R. STARR

❀ Created with Vellum

1

SARA

When you feel you have to triple lock your doors, fumbling with the latch back and forth for minutes, then there's something wrong. When you peek your head through the gap in the venetian blinds at the sign of the first sight of light and you're scared to venture out, then there's something wrong. When you run with fear smothering your lungs from your car to the front door, then there's something wrong. That's how it was for the first few months since my last case. A drain on my mental faculties in the worst way. The uncontrollable flashbacks in the middle of the night haunted my sleep. I woke up drenched in terror sweat. The Viper's face was etched in my subconscious, including his murderous hands yanking his fake dentures free from his slimy mouth. I tried to focus my thoughts on the present. The whispers of the morning breeze through my open kitchen window felt like the Viper calling me from my Maywood home.

"Saraaaaaaa. Sara. I'm not done with you bitch. Saraaaaaa." I'd began to think I'd lost my ever-loving mind.

When I wasn't plagued by those horrific memories, the hedonic ones crept in like a worm burrowing into a sweet apple. I'd tasted the dangerous lips of a billionaire and the naughty imp inside me craved more. It had been six months since the case with Robert Elliot and the reckless man was moving pieces on the chessboard with ease.

I played with the ends of my hair, screwing up my nose as a distraction. I realized I desperately needed a haircut. My ends were so split they looked like they were at a t-junction. Time for a visit to my favorite neighborhood hairdresser. I stood at my kitchen counter like I always did these days, peeping through the window. Pale blue skies graced Maywood. We were smack bang in the middle of spring. Normally my favorite time of year, but not right now. I felt like a caged bird with its wings clipped due to paranoia. You would feel the same if an undesirable assassin was still on the loose and possibly hunting you. Dog walkers were out with their pups, I noted. Nothing salacious. Just your normal everyday routines in Maywood. I let the water boil on the stove as I watched the bubbles come to the surface and simmer out onto my gas stovetop.

"*Shit!*" I exclaimed as the water spilled over onto my tiles. I stepped back to avoid being scalded. I took the pot off the heat and poured into my French press. My head jolted quickly as the sound of my phone vibrating on the counter woke me from my morning reverie.

Homeland Security. "Hi Sara, Dermas here. I wanted to give you an update and check in with you." I pressed the French press down to infuse the grounded coffee together with the hot water. I pushed out a long breath.

"Ok. Great. Go ahead." I sighed hard. I never told them about the note I found from Elliot. In a lot of ways, I was kicking myself about it. The note felt too personal to share. It was mine. Besides if I showed them the note, my penchant for devious men would be uncovered. I imagined the questions would come thick and fast like pepper bullets.

Why did he say you have unfinished business Sara?

Why would he think that?

What aren't you telling us, Sara? Did you have something to do with the murder of Michael Sawyer?

What's your involvement with Robert Elliot?

I imagined the stark white walls of the FBI investigation room caving in on me with two men in black suits interrogating. The heavy breathing, the beads of sweat, the tripping over my inflated tongue. *No.* That secret note stayed with me, under my bed in a shoebox tucked away. I came back to reality listening to Dermas.

"So far we haven't been able to locate Elliot in the city. There's an official manhunt out on him to bring him in for questioning. I'm confident he's skipped town and incognito elsewhere. His company is being operated by the shareholders and no calls or communications have been made in any form or fashion." Dermas's matter-of-fact tone rattled me.

"Has this information been shared by Interpol?" I questioned.

"Yes. He's on the red list. He's officially been listed as a fugitive," Dermas added. My heart thumped in my chest loudly. A fugitive on the run. No way he could outrun this. No way in hell that Elliot could ever return to New York. *Ever.* Right? Why did I have this sinking feeling in my stomach that I was wrong?

"Ok. Thanks for the update. What about the other guy, Clope?" My coffee was well and truly infused. I poured out the brunette liquid into my cup adding a splash of milk. I took a sip and let it slide down my tight throat.

"We have some circumstantial evidence from forensics on him. It's not the first time we've seen Clope. He's got a rap sheet a mile long. Great criminal defense team. He manages to get off every single time. Money talks and bullshit walks; this guy reeks of it. We don't have the murder weapon, which is the problem. Otherwise, we could put the guy under the jail. *But.* What we do have is fibers from the ligature marks around Michael's Sawyers wrists which match the rope type we found when we raided Clope's house. Plus, we have the direct conversations of Elliot admitting to the murder with him. Problem is because of the way the information was obtained then it may not stand up in court when we extradite him."

I sighed deeply. *"If you can extradite him,"* I emphasized. Elliot is going to get away with it again. Now *I'm* a target. He knows about me. I got the Viper and Clope gunning for me. "Did you find anything on files in his house? His chamber? Did you obtain a search warrant?" I asked in a tangled breath.

"I know you're nervous. I can tell. Elliot can't touch you; we expect him to come for you. If he even takes a piss in another country and he's spotted, we're going to bring him in. Clope, too. He's on watch. Elliot is a smart guy – he ain't a billionaire for no reason. His files are impeccable in terms of business paperwork. No trails. It might take us years to unravel if he is laundering money. Clope has legit dealings with Elliot in terms of real estate. So far, we can't find any holes. The Elliot clan have deep connections globally. It's a tough nut to crack. I've been tracking this guy for years waiting for him to slip. We know he had something to do with those drug shipments on the wharf. We ain't got enough on that, though."

I sipped my coffee which I was a third of the way through and walked over to my corkboard. Elliot's face was plastered all over it with pins and information. Connecting the dots, or trying to. "Keep me posted, Dermas. I need a vacation. This shit has me up at night."

Dermas chuckled, a laugh between two weary justice warriors. "Hey, you and me both. My wife thinks I know more about Elliot than our marriage. Shit's crazy. If you even feel like one thing is suspicious, call my direct line. Don't hesitate. Try to stay sane and take that holiday. Sounds like you could do with a sea change, the shit never stops and there will always be another criminal to chase."

I nodded my head silently. The thought had crossed my mind several times. "I know. I can't live my life in fear. I got a few cases piling up. Ever since the newspaper articles and shit leaking to the press with my involvement on the last case, I've had more work than I can throw a stick at."

Dermas laughed again. "Comes with the territory. Listen, I gotta roll, but remember what I said. If you come up with any clues or anything, remember you can hit my line."

I ran my hand through my thick ebony hair. "Yup. I will, thanks, Dermas."

"Bye, Sara," The phone clicked dead. I drained the last of my coffee, scrutinizing my criminal corkboard. It might even be time to look into the family lineage, but that was a Pandora's box and might take me months I didn't have. *Who was behind Elliot?* His father had to know where Elliot was hiding. First, I needed some fresh air to clear out the mental cobwebs.

I stepped out the front door letting the Maywood breeze soothe my nerves. I walked with purpose to Little Birdy Café, my favorite coffee shop of all time. As usual, old school classics pumped through the café when I arrived, taking me back in time. A young dude with a criss cross red and black flannelette shirt and jeans bopped his head to whatever his headphones were playing. Two young giggly girls laughed and pointed to a group of guys out front of the glass windows of the café.

An open face greeted me at the counter.

"Hi Devin, how you doin'?" I smiled. I'd been coming to Little Birdy Café for the last three years and as long as I'd been here Devin had been part of the furniture.

"Hey, Sara. You're kinda famous now, right? I saw you on the news. Some sort of kidnapping with a supermodel, huh?"

he quizzed, as he turned the knobs on the coffee machine. "I know your order. I'll start. Same as usual, right?"

I sighed with irritation. "Yup." My eyes darted around as I cringed at being exposed.

"I don't really want to talk about that case anymore. I've done it to death. I just came in for a coffee," I tried to divert his attention. Devin, unaware of my shame over the matter, lowered his head to concentrate on my coffee order. A red-headed woman with a baby stared at the news, giving me the once over. I gave her a chaste smile. I knew the raspberry patches of heat were rising to the surface of my cheeks.

"Oh. Sorry. I didn't mean to put you on the spot. I just saw it and thought to ask you about it." I put my hand up to stop Devin from talking.

"It's ok. No problem. I'm going to be sitting in my usual spot near the window." I slid over the money at the counter. "Keep the change." I pursed my lips together as I slid into the window seat. Everybody knew about the kidnapping. I pressed my fingers to my temple. The stabbing pain of a stress headache threatened to overtake my eyesight. I lifted my hands out of my pocket and clasped them together in front of me. I focused on the cute little daisies in mason jars in the middle of every table. I moved the mason jar from side to side; my hands needed occupying. The pressure from all the eyes on me made me tighten up. I breathed out slowly as I let my mind drift. Where could I get away from it all? Where could I just breathe and soak up the sun? I jumped up from the table and reached for a magazine out of the rack. Devin brought my hot coffee to the table moments later.

"I'm sorry I overstepped the mark before. I'm sure you've been bombarded by everyone about it all," Devin said smoothly with a grin on his face. I pegged Devin to be in his late twenties. Cute, I'm sure he got plenty of ladies' attention. Devin had both lean arms on the chair opposite me, looking me square in the face. I gazed at his pupils. Dilated. Part of my training I guess. The way he leaned his body over the chair and licked his lips. I knew what was coming. He adjusted the menu on the table before he pounced.

"Hey, it's alright. I'm just over it right now. But it comes with the territory of being a P.I."

Devin hung off my every word and kept gazing at my mouth. I cleared my throat a little, preparing myself to ignore him by looking at the magazine I had in hand. His presence was still there, playing with the menu.

"So hey," Devin said hesitantly.

I placed my lips over the mug, sipping my coffee. "Yes?"

"You've been coming in here a long time and I've never seen you with a guy. Are you single?" He pulled his hand back, looking over his shoulder to his vacant coffee post.

I tilted my head at him a little. "Yes, I am. Don't remind me," I mumbled. Instantly Robert's hard body pressing against me in the café eclipsed my mind. I closed my eyes briefly to erase him.

"I ah… wondered if you would like to go out with me sometime? Just like… go listen to some music or something. Do you like bands?"

I gazed one more time at Devin. Couldn't hold a candle to Elliot. I placed my mug down.

Maybe I should go, might take my mind off things with Robert.

"Sure, why not? And yes – I like bands," I smiled warmly at him.

His grin turned up a thousand watts. "Great. I uh... got a pen here. Can you write your number down?" He grabbed the pen from behind his ear and ripped a piece of paper from his notepad.

I looked up at him through my lashes. "Ok." I wrote my number down on the piece of paper and gave it to him. No harm.

He stuffed it in his pocket and winked. "I'll give you a call soon, Sara."

Not knowing what to do with my hands I hung onto my mug for security purposes. "Ok."

What did I just agree to? In my mind it couldn't be any worse than the cop that asked me to go fishing with him and his buddies. Tuh.

2

ELLIOT

"They ain't got nothing. Can't touch me boss," Clope's raspy voice replied cockily.

"You on the burner phone?" I asked lightly. I had to be sure. If the feds traced the call, he just made it harder for me. I was in front of a world class view, a landscape postcard on steroids. I was calling my right-hand man to feel out the situation.

"No doubt, what do you take me for boss? I been at this a minute. I ain't let you down yet," Clope, my clean-up guy, responded.

"You damn sure have been close, Clope," I warned. I let the seaside air hit the open vessel of my chest. I had a few buttons undone with a Henny on the rocks in front of me. I swirled the amber liquid around in the glass thinking over my next assault on the world.

Clope's raspy Boston laugh boomed through the phone. "You ain't got nothing to worry about, boss. I got you. By the way, that property on Long Island went through sweet. Smooth deal. You up six mil on that one." Clope, my undertaker, was doing good work for the most part. I just had to bide my time long enough to slip back into New York and resume the throne. Looking out over the still crystalline waters with the gleam of light dancing like diamonds, I knew Portugal could be a blessing in disguise. A new arm of my operational expansion was coming into view. As an Elliot, we didn't stay down or out of sight for long.

"Good, that's what I like to hear. Evana? You got any leads?" I pressed.

"Nah. Nothing yet. I'm on it. That Viper guy disappeared, too. We paid that son of a bitch handsomely."

"Leave that one alone. Safe to say we're not hiring him again," I replied sarcastically. I flicked my Rolex over on my wrist while the sun hit my toned athletic legs. I would have to move from people watching as they were starting to burn a little.

"You got that right. Evana is long gone. I don't know where but if she's in New York the toaster is on for her. Know what I mean?" Clope threatened.

I let a throaty laugh escape. "Yeah, I know what you mean. I give it a couple of years. I gotta clear the air here and talk to Pops; I need a defense attorney. Let's see if I can get the same one OJ Simpson had. Look into it for me," I ordered.

Clope was as deftly deceitful and built for the crime game as me. We were a good one-two combo. "Boss, you're a wild one. If they only knew," he added.

I held my glass up to that sentiment from my end. "If they only knew Clope. *If only*. Let's keep that between you and me. We got bigger fish to fry. Find out about the Columbians. The Pecador crew. I know they probably got a hit out on me for delivering a dud satellite."

"Yeah. I'm not gonna lie on that one. You're going to need an army. I'm working on it from my end."

"Good and I got some allies in place that will back me up. Some deals I'm setting up right now. It's going to work out. It's all about strategy, baby. How are you holding up? Feds pressing you?" I let the amber liquid loosen up tension in my veins. I was in the mood for some partying and I knew just the spot to take it to.

"I mean yeah. But they can't touch me, they don't have the evidence to force a conviction or nuthin'" Clope sounded confident but given the years he'd been running from the law I knew anything could change at any minute. Hence the slight deviation in plan to the capital of Portugal, Lisbon. I've been here many times. Built some solid relationships of all kinds. The least I could do was reward the getaway with a party. As the soft billowy winds of Portugal drifted by, my mind opened to the hot detective. Ms. Clemens. Those soft rose-stained lips. I longed to taste them again, to have her buckle at the knees from my touch. It would only be a matter of time. My phone reverberated on the plastic table in front of me as I watched the sea waves lick the shoreline.

"Hullo," I answered sharply.

"Boa tarde. We meet at Rua Moeda say four horas," a gravelly voice commanded through the other end of the line.

"Está bem, brother," I responded.

"Are you ready to party? We got some nice girls for you," the caller switched to English.

I flexed my legs out in olive-skinned long-legged beauty in a white bikini passing by. I leaned forward, dropping my sunglasses from my nose following her tight perky ass. It bounced in perfect timing as she walked. She flicked me a wink over her shoulder. As soon as I lifted them back on my face, Sara's perfectly sculpted body flashed in front of my eyes. I was simmering with untapped heat as I peered at my near empty glass. She was like a beautiful nightmare that wouldn't leave my mind. I intended to shake the memory loose, just for tonight. I drained the droplets of my Henny, ending my seaside jaunt.

I had a penthouse arrangement organized with the hotel owner, Piedre. Same place I've been staying for years. A glorious hideout hidden in plain view. A white villa palace fit for a king with maids at my beck and call. I walked through the reception area where million-dollar artwork hung on the walls, I and smirked to myself. I sure knew how to pull off a double cross. Homeland Security would be pulling their hair out knowing they couldn't have me; as always, I had my shady connections.

As I entered my villa, a young sexy maid in a black and white outfit entered. "Señor. Can I do anything for you?" she asked a little too eagerly.

"Yes. Can you ring Ricardo?" I took off my sunglasses off and front of me. "That works for me. I'm always ready if the circumstances are right," I replied.

"Good. Good. See you there." A little Portuguese is what I knew, enough to mingle with the locals and my business associates. Got me over the line often enough.

I clicked off the call. Another meeting with a prominent drug lord. Since Portugal's decriminalization policy on drugs it'd been much easier to set up my operation here.

I lifted my glass up to her and ran my eyes blatantly over her smooth legs. She blushed a little and re-adjusted. "Just admiring the view. No need to be shy," I coaxed smoothly. I loved pouring on my famous Elliot charm.

"Thank you. Anything else?" Her broken accent was extremely appealing; she's one I wanted to test run later on.

"Hmm... let me see. My shirt needs ironing. Can you do that for me, sweetie?" I flicked some folded U.S. dollars her way. She quickly grabbed it as if there was no more.

"No need to worry. Plenty more where that came from as long as you keep me... satisfied," I advised with amusement.

Her cute dimples mixed with her olive-kissed skin made for a nice piece of eye candy. She giggled behind her hand. "You are silly, Señor."

"Hmm. I've been called other things, a lot worse actually, but I'll take it." I slipped out of my shirt unveiling my toned torso and well-cut chest. I'd been consistently staying in shape my whole life. Helped me stay one step ahead of everyone else in the game and allowed me to settle some of the raging testosterone in my system. I averted my eyes to gauge the maid's reaction before she left the room. She moistened her lips in desire, just like they all do.

"Oh my," she fanned herself and I grinned. She closed the large rounded doors behind her. An underhanded smile tugged at the edges of my mouth. Another warm pussy to run through. *Later...*

I left her wide-mouthed. As I moved around the villa to the expansive bathroom, a small problem plagued me. *Evana.* My runaway wife who I failed to kill. She was like an annoying mosquito that needed swatting. I stroked my chin. A little prickly around the edges, I located my razor to rectify it as the maid softly re-entered behind me.

"Ah, sir. Your shirt is here. I lay it on the bed for you," she bowed graciously. I continued to evaluate my stubble. I turned to ask for her opinion as she collected my clothes for dry cleaning.

"Yes or no?" I caressed my jaw as she folded my belongings in the laundry bag.

"Bonito!" she said softly, which means 'beautiful' in Portuguese. I guess the stubble will stay. "Your transportation is waiting downstairs for you," she added. Seemed most speak broken Portuguese here. Perhaps they're indulging me. Or maybe not. All of her eye-fluttering is good for my inflated ego. She moved her petite hourglass frame out of the two-story villa before I had time to cultivate my seductive prowess. I looked around and saw the villa was bathed in white and cream with tasteful ornaments strategically placed around the space. The chandeliers that hung were a sensual treat for the eyes at nighttime with their golden hue. They added an old-world glamor feel. The winding white bannisters both inside and outside possessed intricate European designs carved into them. I slid on my gold Rolex, dabbed a little cologne behind my ears, and finished with a minimal amount of gel through my hair. One last glance in the mirror before heading downstairs to the car. Not bad. Not bad at all.

"Ricardo! My man. You're looking good. Long time no see." I dapped him up, shifting into the back of the vehicle as he held the door open.

"Yes, boss – I agree," Ricardo reiterated. He was my Portuguese driver who picked me up in a black town car for blending purposes. I didn't mind slumming it every now and again. In New York I had a limo driver. Got to work with what you got sometimes.

"We are headed to Café Janis, yes?" he asked with a light accent.

"Right we are, my friend. How's family life? Your little girls were just heading to school last time I was here," I noted.

"Yes. That's right. Good memory, Roberto. That was a while back now. Right after you bought the warehouses, right?"

"Yes, that's right. You have a good memory also." My sunglasses were on as I let my gaze wander along the Portuguese suburbs.

"Haha. We had some fun times then. You entertained a lot of people." Ricardo winked in the mirror.

My eyes twinkled from the memories of classic parties, women in hot tubs, torrid sex affairs and plenty of blow. I shrugged my head, I'd definitely lived.

Now, I had heat on me in New York. Another memory surfaced... Cluster Ferman. He was found slumped behind the containers in a standard execution-style hit. Evana's father and confidant. I brought her to Portugal for our first ever international jaunt as man and wife after that incident. To ease the pain of the death I caused... that she didn't know of at the time. I remembered ordering the hit clear as day.

"Take him out. He's not complying."

"Yes boss. Nice and clean. Then you got control of the docks, right?"

"Right."

The vivid memory melded together with all the other violent acts. Once I organized one hit, it made it easy for the next targets. Then it became a habit for a guy like me.

As the streets of Portugal merged into a blur en route to Café Janis, I wondered if Evana coming up missing was karmic payback. Had to admit Ms. Clemens did good to keep her out of harm's way. I don't know how she did it. Something told me she had help. I stroked my chin with one finger. Too many elements would make it hard for her to be operating solo. As I tossed the ball around on it, Café Janis came into view.

Very low key, not a high society venue at all. People jostled for space in the vibrant day café. Students with backpacks, men and women in all shapes and colors, I would call them chic. Very European in flavor and design. I placed my sunglasses on my head as Ricardo dropped me off and I walked into the all-day breakfast café. Nothing like Manhattan constituents where black and grey are staple outfit colors. I'm drawn into a customary European hug and handshake as soon as I'm spotted.

"Roberto! You make it. Come, we sit and talk shop," a slight upbeat tan-skinned man beckoned me to a table of five. One was wearing a beret and a sweater vest. The other three were dressed casually also. The one thing we all had in common is that we were cold blooded killers and drug kingpins in our respective countries.

3

SARA

♟

Late Friday night, and not even the guy *I didn't* want to call wasn't calling. I'd written my number down reluctantly on that napkin over a week ago. Maybe Devin just wanted to clout chase so he could show his friends he could pull an investigator. After all, I'd been all over the news for the last little bit.

I peered down at myself. A few stray crumbs were making a trail down my stomach from the cheese and crackers was gorging myself on. My long dark hair was in better shape as I'd gone to my hairdresser. Pity it wouldn't stay this sleek and shiny. Never could keep the style for long once I left. She agreed that I needed a vacation as well.

"Gurl, you better get that coochie serviced before it disappears. Maybe you should try one of those S.W.A.T. guys. They look damn good in uniform." She was sassy with a big Afro and always dishing out the local dirt.

"I heard Chandra got together with one of them and ooo honeyyy, she raved about it. Put the handcuffs on her and all." She made a gyrating gesture as she combed through my locks, had me in

fits of laughter. She successfully held down the gossip lane in Maywood.

"*You're right. Shit is sad,*" I lamented.

I was on my couch with a glass of red and a comedy movie that wasn't holding my interest. Not the worst evening, but not the best ever. Hawk was somewhere in Istanbul chasing criminals. He called to check in from time to time.

"Hey you. How are you holding up?"

"As best I can. Feel icky in my apartment. Clope is nowhere near being brought in so I feel like a failure in my job," I confessed.

"Chin up. It's not over yet. I got a feeling Elliot is going to make himself known soon enough. You'll get another chance to nail him. Clope will slip. The guy's a highly paid thug. They *always* slip, they get cocky," Hawk stressed.

"Thanks for the encouragement. Say hi to Evana for me. I can't believe you guys are together," I said. Shit was weird.

"I hear you. Crazier to me than you. But it's working. I will let her know. She's safer with me than anything, given Elliot's going to come looking for her. It's only a matter of time. If she stays with me, I can keep her from being detected. Make sure you hit my phone if shit goes down," he warned.

"*Soooo*, are you only with her because you can keep her safe?" I questioned him.

"Not on the tongue of hell's breath would I do that. You know me better than that."

I grimaced; Hawk used to be known for his detachment with women. "You're right. You must really love her. You've changed," I laughed, teasing him.

"I do. Why do you think I was so invested in your case?" he added.

"Ahhhh! So, the truth comes out now. *That's why*. I had a feeling at the beginning when you asked me about her being in love with Elliot. I thought it was strange."

Hawk's wry chuckle filtered through the phone. "My poker face was showing. I had to see how hard it would be to steal my girl back didn't I?"

I laughed. "I would expect nothing less, Hawk." I sat up a little. "Good luck with your mark."

"No luck needed," I felt him grinning. A small smile came over my lips from the memory. Hawk, a slick heavy-duty assassin of his own breed and one of the baddest in the business. Highly sought after. Hence, the Istanbul run. I shook my head at the thought of his assassin journey. The fact we were connected was something out of this world.

"Ok bad boy see you later," I said quickly.

I grabbed the remote and flicked through the channels, the rom com wasn't cutting it. I stopped as the glint of turquoise water caught my sleepy eyes. A commercial ad. I found myself swaying in time with the ad's music as it took me on a journey through Portugal's city to the countryside. I sat up, interested, bunching up my pajamas in excitement.

Tickets to Lisbon Portugal are now on sale. Experience the real Europe. Get in quick! Book in now and receive two nights free at the hotel of your choice...

I DROPPED the cracker I'd been munching on from my mouth and wiped the crumbs. *Yes!* That's where I needed to go. Hot Brazilian and Portuguese guys, sunshine, oceans and exquisite architecture. Not to mention succulent, mouth-watering Portuguese tarts. I dusted myself off, scrambling to my laptop before my logical brain kicked in telling me to stop. I pried it open and without thinking, promptly booked a two-week holiday to Portugal. My clients would have to wait. I didn't have any hardcore cases anyway. A small twinge of guilt hit me as I thought of Michael's father and the promise I made him.

"I WANT *you to bring Elliot down. No matter what it takes. I will avenge my son's death and you're the woman to help me do it."*

FUCK IT – avengers need a break, too. I desperately craved something to look forward to in life. All this tossing and turning, double and triple locking was setting me up for the looney bin. Satisfied and slightly excited, I got up and started dancing one foot to the other, bouncing around and flinging my hands up. Hawk would've been proud. Something close to what his ancestors would do.

Portugal, here I come!

The excitement faded rapidly, morphing into caution. A loud crashing sound put me on high alert. I froze in the middle of my living room. My head and my body rooted to the spot while I assessed my next motion. I padded softly towards the sound. I shakily opened my kitchen drawer retrieving my loaded Smith and Wesson. I gripped it tightly, my lips drier than unspread toast. I pulled the venetians open near the kitchen with the tip of my gun. Pure ebony night, stars were littering the sky. Neighbors houses were lit up with golden lights, people were enjoying their Friday nights in. With my gun sheltered low in both hands, I kicked open my screen door.

The sharp Jersey breeze rushed in.

Left to right, my head swiveled.

No clue of the noises' origins.

BUT... I knew I heard something...

My low squat was so no one would see my gun cocked. I

didn't want the neighbors to think I was about to perform a mass shooting.

Meooow. To my left two little glowing eyes stared back at me through the dark. I clutched my shirt front, bunching it up in relief.

I released the breath that I'd held in. *Damn cat.* I narrowed my eyes, looking closer. As the animal slinked towards me, I saw it was a fat ginger cat.

"Meckles... You scared the living shit out of me. Come here," I chastised, beckoning the cat to me. Meckles, my neighbor's cat from the across the road, had come to pay me a visit.

"Was that you banging around out here?" I scratched him behind the ears as he purred, closing his eyes and rubbing against my hand. "Was that you?" I asked again, as if the cat could talk. I patted his soft fur and the purring increased. "You should get back to your owners instead of roaming the neighborhood," I whispered. Meckles just looked at me with his cute face, continuing to press his head into my hand for more pats. As I let go of the acute terror, I released Meckles, his tail swinging a couple of times. Once he realized he wasn't getting any more pats, he tiptoed away. I closed the screen and went back inside. Yup. I had to leave the country, right along with this paranoia.

I stepped back inside, lowering my gun, resting it on the table for a minute. The booking was two days away. I just had to keep my delusions at bay long enough to board the plane. My sleeping patterns were off, so I made my way to packing. I flipped on my bedroom light, starting the process of dragging my dusty suitcase out from the bottom of the closet. I covered my mouth, balking at the amount of dust particles flying around. I shook my head pitifully. I didn't want an onslaught of sneezing to be added to the mix. The last time I'd been on holiday was three years ago with my ex-boyfriend, Tory. I shifted my memory back to Cancun.

Most people were half-naked the whole time; sunshine, Mojitos, swimming pools, friendly people and parties galore. Tory, though, had a little too much fun…

"*Ahh, just like that.* This is how you Spanish women do it? Oh yeah… That's perfect."

We'd been at the bar in Cancun having a good time. I let loose a little more pre-private investigator days. I'd gone looking for Tory.

"Babe! Wait 'til you see-" I had my fourth Mojito in my hand. He hadn't heard me. I'd tiptoed quietly to the unisex toilet. My ear was cocked to the door. I retreated back a little so I could peer under the door. Tory's underwear and colorful shorts were around his ankles. Two knees were on the other side of Tory's toned calves with a whole lot of slurping noises going on.

I banged hard on the door. "What the fuck is going on in there!" I was a little drunk and vocal.

"Oh shit!" his panicked voice said. The underwear shot up and so did the shorts in a flash.

"What the hell do you think is going on in here?" A Spanish accent spat back angrily. My mouth dropped open, my head swirling from too many Mojitos at the bar.

The door swung wide open as a guilty-looking Tory stared back at me. A good-looking Spanish woman with wild hair pushed past me, glaring. "He's all yours." My glass slipped clean out of my fingers and smashed onto the ground shattering, leaving the mint leaves in the center.

"You piece of shit," I'd spat back with a twisted, hurt face.

His palms faced out as his shoulders hunched up in the guiltiest-looking face I'd ever seen. "It's not what it looks like. I promise you," he pleaded with his sneaky eyes.

I turned on my heel, packed my shit from the hotel room and checked out on a plane straight home. In a lot of ways going on this trip would heal the past and give me fresh new memories to put in my catalogue.

I shifted back to the present, opening my suitcase and taking off the tag from my last trip to Mexico. As I packed, I put outfits in and took them out.

What if I meet a hot Brazilian? I want to have a beautiful dress, right? Hmm... Speaking of Brazilian... a wax might be in order before I leave.

Soon my bedroom was filled like a floordrobe. Disheartened with the mess I'd made and a little tired, I laid back, letting myself drift to sleep with the light on. Must have been hours, or at least it felt like hours, when my eyes fluttered open in pitch darkness.

Did the light blow out? I didn't remember turning the light out... I touched myself. My body was good, not touched.

My heart thumped loudly in my chest as I clutched both hands to the bed linen.

I gasped for air. *What the fuck?*

I scrambled to the edge of the bed, knees knocking together and touched the light switch. The light flicked on.

I covered my mouth as raspy breaths filled my clogged lungs.

I know for a fact I didn't turn the light switch off. *I'd fallen asleep with it on.*

I scanned my eyes around the room. The bedroom window was shut tight.

I honed in on it, running my fingers along the windowsill for any sign of entry.

None.

I touched the door, which was open, nothing.

I dropped to the floor to see if clothes were out of place. No. They were in the same place I left them. My stomach retracted a little as I stepped over the clothes. I'd been complacent, my Smith and Wesson wasn't in the drawer where I normally left it. I'd placed it on the kitchen counter carelessly. I ran to it. Sliding it off the counter accidentally, I reached to pick it up. I watched as it clunked on my new timber board floor. *Shit. Shit. Shit.* I couldn't live like this. I slid down the kitchen cabinet, bursting into tears. I placed my head in my hands. I would become a prisoner in my own home if I didn't do something, and all because of my own silent fears.

Minutes later I rose up from the floor, calling Hawk. Couldn't call my parents, they already didn't want me to be a P.I. and this would just be the reinforcement they needed for me to stop. I moistened my dry lips as I punched in Hawk's number. The international dial tone clicked in and he answered.

"Hey sugar plum," he said cheerfully.

"Hey Hawk."

"You sound glum. What's going on?" A rapid clicking sound pervaded through the phone.

"What *are* you doing?"

"I am..." I heard him straining and gritting his teeth. "I am on this mark's ass and I'm changing rounds is all. I'm in disguise right now, Istanbul style. You should see it. You would be impressed."

I let a rare giggle escape my lips. Hawk had a way about him to lift my spirits. "Wow. You're right – that's something I would love to see. Send me a picture," I said trying to move my mind elsewhere.

"You bet your sweet legs I will. Evana sends her love. She's modeling in Paris right now."

I lit up at the news, "I'm just glad she's safe. That's great," I remarked.

Again, I poked around my apartment for a sign of human entry, but couldn't find any. "Hawk, I feel scared and paranoid. I heard a noise outside and saw it was my neighbor's cat. I thought I went to sleep with my light on and it was off when I woke up. I don't know what to do." I let the fears rush out of me.

Radio feedback cut through at Hawk's end. "You know what I think?"

"What's that?"

"I think you need a vacation. But before you do that. Check your bedroom window again. Go to it now," Hawk commanded.

My heart rate quickened. "Funny you should say that. I've just booked a vacay to Portugal for two weeks to decompress." I pivoted and walked to my bedroom; Hawk continued.

"Ahh. My old stomping ground, Portugal. Nice country. Maybe I can meet you there. Are you at your window yet?"

"Yes, I am now..." I ran my finger over my bedroom window, which sat behind my bed facing east. On the right-hand corner, I noticed the paint chipped away with the timber slightly splintered. You would need to blink to see it. Maybe. Just one tiny split of timber. My hands started to tremble, and the water formed in the pockets of my eyes. "Hawk."

"Yes?"

"There's a splinter in the bottom right hand corner, I can't be sure if it was there before. It's an old house and the window frames aren't in the best of condition. Fuck."

"Send me the shot of it now. Call Dermas. Get him in there. Head to Portugal so they can sweep the place. Take every precaution, just in case."

"Alright," I replied shakily.

"Sara, ring him, then call me back. When's your flight out?"

"In two days," I said, working to gulp down the lump forming in my throat.

"Ok. Can you go to your parent's place?"

I felt the anger bubbling up inside of me. "If it is the Viper, I'm not letting him run me out of my fucking home. That's for sure."

Hawk paused. "Alright. But tell Dermas, I'm not there. If I

have a vision about it, I'll call you and you have to follow what I tell you. Got it?"

"I trust that, but for now I'm staying put," I cemented.

"Roger that. Right now, I have the mark in sight and I gotta nail him." Hawk said quietly.

"Ok, do your thing." I let Hawk go from the call.

"Bye. Trust your instincts. I trust yours," Hawk said clearly. I punched in Homeland Security's number.

4

ELLIOT

"We've been waiting for you, friend," came the warm greeting from a revered Columbian drug cartel leader, Fabio Coron Vasquez. A middle-aged gentleman, he sported dark hair, leathery olive skin and was dressed in a tan leather jacket, jeans and a white t-shirt. His leather loafers spelled wealth, and his look was topped off with a white Cuban hat. His black obsidian eyes held a reflective shine that mirrored the darkness he harbored. I knew. I'd had dealings with him before. He tipped his hat for me to sit down. I shook the other men's hands looking them all in the eye.

My father used to tell me. *"Always look your enemy in the eye before you fuck them. Never back down."* A lesson I never forgot.

Loud, animated European chatter surrounded us. A red Vespa pulled up outside of the café and two young people jumped off. I was used to this level of hustle and bustle as a New Yorker, and in being a frequent visitor to Portugal.

"Pleasure to be here gentlemen," I said cordially as I took

a seat. On the table was a large jug of pisco sour in the middle of the table along with a tasting platter.

"Would you like a glass before we get down to business?" The older man from Mexico with the sweater vest gestured as I settled into the groove of the bright yellow couch.

"Yes, fill me up," I replied simply. He poured the mustard-colored cocktail into a low glass for me. I raised the sour-tasting liquid to my lips, flinching as the sweet bitterness hit my taste buds in a rude way.

All of them laughed at my response. "Hey, nothing like this Peruvian number. I love it." I raised my glass as did the others and we clinked together in unison.

The Peruvian drug lord - Juan Galvez, a handsome bald-headed man in his thirties, responded. "Come to my country, we will show what other drinks we have. This is nothing. Like water. We have something that will knock the leather off your jacket." His mouth twisted in a menacing way as he flicked his hand off at the weakness of the pisco sours.

"I'm sure," I replied smoothly.

"Gentleman. We all know why we're here." The Mexican, Donte Guzman, the leader of the group, spoke. His surprisingly warm eyes met and levelled with all of ours. "We have an opportunity to take our operations to the next level. All of you know my history and my involvement with the Pistoleros; that was long ago. You could say this is a network or a brother company to that." The men chuckled at the reference. "We were ruthless in our time, now we need to get a little slicker in our dealings," he added. He rubbed his ringed, chubby fingers together. Pure gold sat on three of them. "Elliot has been brought in to manage the setup of our expansion into American headquarters. I will let Elliot tell you about it. Go ahead, brother."

I cracked my knuckles before I began. "Well let me start by saying, I'm in a predicament which can be rectified. I'm sure you've seen the news. However, I have New York on a nice set of benefits." The table laughed. "My operation is still running smoothly. On a fortnightly basis we pull in around $10 million -that's after payment of staff. I'm no Pablo Escobar, but with the power of all our networks I believe we can triple our income. I require a level of protection as the Pecadora Cartel are salty about the recent satellite loss. I made some nice pocket change from that deal. Naturally they want their money back. I have sole ownership of the warehouse docks in New York. Our operational expansion is now imminent. What I require is the ability to move freely with extradition treaties and laws from your countries. My numbers predict that together we can increase our profits by 40-60% if done right. My family line has been dealing with all of you or your direct ancestors for centuries." I paused for effect and looked them all in the eye. "We wish to continue the brotherhood in a civil way."

Fabio drained the majority of his pisco sours, nodding. "We have all in all, minus a few mishaps, good dealings," Fabio stated carefully. He crossed his leg over and spread his arms across the back of the couch revealing the tattoos under his armpits. Those 'mishaps' resulted in 50 deaths between camps. But hey, no harm no foul. I nodded in appreciation.

Donte Guzman, the kind-looking Mexican who ran a $10 million a week operation through his cartel spoke. "Well, we have been beefing with the Pecadora crew for years. Give me the names and we'll monitor the situation. They would be fools to start a war now... One of their own recently got indicted for money laundering." The kind eyes didn't change, but the evil smile with the gold tooth cap gave way to his ruthlessness. Donte kept talking as we snacked. "Either that or we send word to have them kept out of the way. They don't have the manpower and reach our cartel does. They will respect it. So, Elliot, that's not an issue." The animation of his speech went up a notch as he announced, "Now let's get down to the nitty gritty. Elliot, we are interested in the way in which you run your port. We can all learn here." Donte's eyes flicked up to the group, who were listening intently. The world around us kept on. People came and went with their orders. I picked up a Portuguese tart from the plate, biting into its rich sugary goodness.

I loved a good speech. "The way I figure, we are in a good position due to the Portuguese's decriminalization laws. We can work through the ships, Miguel. I know you have strong links to the wharf here. Fabio, your pure product will blow them away and it's a third of the price of regular blow in New York. My network are players of two mil and up to billionaires. We can hike the price four times over and they won't blink an eye. Welcome to New York, fellas – my city," I said with a cocky smile. The adrenaline surged through my crooked veins as I frothed at the mouth at the promise of immeasurable power to come. Having an air of invincibility made my dick hard.

Fabio gave me a wary stare. "Tell us more about the port operation." He picked up a toothpick from the table, picking between his teeth.

I complied, raising my voice over the background noise. "We have a foreman at each warehouse who checks all shipments. I have connections at all the ports we regularly run through. He sends me the manifest ahead for the week, letting me know if certain shipments have come in. Of course, I know they're coming. That's the communication that *we* will have. He organizes a driver who we pay handsomely to deliver to a specific warehouse location, my distribution team comes in, picks up their cut, works the streets and we collect. Nice, simple, easy and clean. We have connections in customs, air, sea and land. I got New York on lock. Political officials are in; cops, lawyers, drivers, celebs – the works," I said with a cocksure knowing. "It's going to be a process to bed it down, six months to get our flow right. If I worked the numbers right, I see an increase of at least $5 million a week each. *Easy.* Unlimited potential for us all."

Juan Galvez, the lady killer with mocha colored skin and a shiny bald dome, chimed in. "In Peru, we make the product from local coca growers, the richest soil." He put his hands to his mouth indicating the sweetness that is cocaine. "Sacred mountain soil does something to the coke. Gives it that extra oomph, you know what I mean?" Juan grinned from ear to ear. "Along with Fabio, we believe we have the cleanest, most pure product there is. It will get you higher than a kite." Juan demonstrated a kite flying through the wind and we all broke into laughter at the table. The afternoon sun was still shining bright through the open-air windows and a hive of activity surrounded us. All the necessary players I needed were at the table.

I carried on with my speech. "That's what the people want. Since we sell at around $30k a kilo, there's some serious money to be had. We just have to secure our shipping cargo network. Keep them happy – that's how this is going to work. As you move the product to me, I open my networks and we can move into, say, Connecticut at least"

"We can't move into Boston? It's a larger city," Juan asked as he cradled his cigar, lighting it up.

"We got some heavy hitting mafia in Boston, so that's tricky territory. That's a longer process of negotiation. They have their set people in place. Down South, now *that's* lucrative. It's a wild man's game down there. Miami. You might have heard of it," I smirked as I responded to Juan.

Donte squeezed my shoulder with a devilish grin. "You're a funny man. A city built off my forefathers. Now that's a city we can run, boys. I know it inside out. I can ease you into new networks and help with that process. A few sit downs here and there," Donte moved his hands side to side as he spoke softly.

I responded, "Perfect. And the west coast quarters, I'm

opening up starting with Hollywood. My foot is firmly in the door boys. Everybody in agreement?" I asked in a firm tone.

As a master of negotiation, I knew who, what, why, and when at the table.

Fabio Coron Vesquez was the Columbian grower and supplied over 40% of Colombia's drug trade. The rival growers – the Pecadora gang – were sitting around 20%, and on the come up. Hence the rivalry. Fabio's loyalty and love of his family, including Columbia, would prove an asset to me. I planned to infiltrate his network to learn more. My Peruvian, Juan Galvez was definitely a snake charmer with fiendish smile, and those blue eyes would make him a pillow talker if I wanted to learn his secrets. I would just pay a woman to break him down. As I observed him, he had his eye on a nice piece of ass walking to the counter.

He slapped his brother Fabio. "She's nice. I gotta go talk to her." He licked his lips sticking out his long tongue. His silk emerald green shirt and white playboy shorts gave him away.

My local Portuguese guy, Miguel Herrera, was the most dangerous to me. He didn't speak much – which made me nervous. "Miguel. My brother, what do you think about the deal?" I smiled wide baring my teeth; only I knew he was dancing with the devil himself.

With his quiet dark eyes, conservative features and poker face I sensed he was observing me like I was observing him. *Smart*. The most unassuming of them all. Miguel was in his late forties. I knew he'd quietly built a small fortune in arms dealing and the drug trade. "I think it can work. As you said we need to secure the port. I have some links, and some officials which can assist with your treaty arrangements. See no evil, hear no evil – that type of thing." He raised his pisco sour and slammed it down. He didn't look directly at me; he looked straight ahead and out into the street.

"Sounds like we've made the first step to a fruitful partnership," I said coolly.

"One part is left." Donte looked around at everyone in the group. All men listened with respect when he spoke. "The oath we take today. If for any reason one of us should get caught, no snitching. If you want out, let's have a conversation. We're all successful men here and there's no need for bloodshed. Let's keep our hands clean and get this dinero together. We shake on it. Here and now."

We all shook hands and a solemn oath was taken, no paperwork, no trails, these relationships were built on years' worth of trust.

"Fucking A," Juan said as a plume of tobacco smoke wafted through the air. "Yo, Elliot, you partying with us tonight? We got some hot ass girls in this part of town; they will do anything you want. And I mean *anything*." He grinned, bobbing his thick eyebrows up and down.

I smiled. "Send me the details. Might swing in for a few." He reached across the table and I opened my palm for a dap. In my mind I already had my sights set on the hot maid for the night.

"My man. You're here for two years, you might as well enjoy. Indulge a little. I'll send a plane ticket for you to come see the plantation. See how we do it," he promised.

"I'm in. Gentlemen it's been a pleasure, but I have some things to take care of. Juan, I might see you later tonight."

"Later, Elliot." He lifted his chin slightly, blowing out smoke from his cigar. The hot bite of the European sun had dissipated, in its place a cooler atmosphere which made it just right for strolling the narrow streets and people watching. I turned back to see all the men still sitting there except for Miguel. As I left, he exited as well taking his lightweight jacket from the back of the couch. From his fleet-footed exit, I gathered he seemed to be in a hurry. I kept my eyes on him as I saw a jet-black Mercedes pick him up and drive off. I made a call on my phone.

"Ricardo, I'm ready to come home."

"Ok, boss, on the way," Ricardo responded. The Mercedes sped away as I looked after it with my hands in my pocket. Miguel Herrera would be one man I needed to learn more about, and quickly.

The iconic architecture with all of its history, intricacies, craftsmanship and flair in Europe blew me away every time. I strolled away from Café Janis to the other side of the road to admire. Conceptually different to the cold, sleek, modern day buildings of Manhattan. I knew it would take Ricardo over 15 minutes to get here. I walked with my hands in my pockets, stepping out into the sweetness of the afternoon and waited. A tall, tanned beauty on a vintage pushbike rode past, twinkling her fingers at me. My lips curved to a smile. Ah, Europe and I were about to have a beautiful love affair. It wasn't long after Ricardo swung into view. I jumped in the back and poured a real drink from the bar. Ricardo lifted his chin and looked at me through the front rearview mirror.

"Good meeting boss?" He asked as he drove off from the curb.

"Yes. Slight little hitch," I replied.

I poured the caramel colored liquid in the crystal tumbler. Ricardo raised an eyebrow,

"Oh yeah? What kind of hitch?"

"What do you know about Miguel Herrera?" I posed.

I watched Ricardo's eyes in the mirror, the edges of his smile curved into a wide-open grin.

"Miguel. Tough, he's well known here. Respected. Knows a lot of people. I've driven for him a time or two. He has extensive links in arms dealing, but you didn't hear that from me. Has all the heavy artillery and deep networks, globally."

"Hmm. Do me a favor... Think you can pick him up a few times? Keep an ear out for me?"

"Done," Ricardo said without question.

As we rode back to the villa, I let my mind take its course and sipped on my drink. The caramel liquid fire hitting my throat, putting me in the mood for an early night, after the maid. That spark of wanting to party left me. I drained the last of my drink and soon enough we reached the villa.

"Thanks Ricardo." I slapped a large roll of bills into his hand and he smiled, tucking it in his pocket. He knew what it meant.

"Anytime boss. See you tomorrow." I slid out of the sleek town car and with my usual cocky swagger entered the whitewashed stone villa entrance. As I opened and folded out the doors, I let the sultry balmy breeze blow through my apartment. I walked to my balcony and looked out over the streets of Portugal. Same place I'd come after the university hustle incident. Same place I'd come after many unfortunate incidents. A standing arrangement after murder.

I let the breeze roll over my face; no better feeling than having the world at your feet. *Except I didn't have it all.* One person eluded my grasp. *Sara Clemens.* My cock rose to attention as soon as I thought about her. I tried to tell myself it was primal, the normal procedure for me to get my needs met, but that was a lie and I knew it.

I walked through the apartment and called room service. "Hi, can I have Isabella come in here? I need a couple of things dropped off for the morning."

"No problem. We will send her right away," the man at the reception said.

I took my shirt off to give her the introduction. Would be tough for her to run from me. Once I poured my ravenous tongue between her silken folds she would be in the palm of my hand and do anything I wanted. Never failed.

"Ola, Elliot –" She arrived at my villa door moments later. I watched her reaction as she recognized I was shirtless. The white curtains were blowing in the breeze behind me and it lifted her chocolate tendrils, blowing them around her sensual face. Her maid outfit hugged all the right curves, perfect for me to bend her over on the bed. As I walked to her an image flashed, Sara's lips in the doorway at the coffee shop. The intense connection we had. In confusion, I shook it off, trying to concentrate on the maid in front of me.

"You work out. Nice," she said, her gaze shifting greedily over my body.

"You like what you see Mami?" I replied huskily.

She giggled in nervousness, ignoring my question. "You called me, what can I do for you? Do you need something cleaned or taken somewhere?" Her flirty tone and the licking of her lips let me know she was ready.

"How about you take a load off and join me for dinner?" I suggested.

Her facial features changed for a few moments. "Señor, I have a job to do and I have to get back. I will get into trouble," she said with apprehension written on her face.

I picked up my phone from the cherry wood table, staring her straight in her pretty brown eyes.

"Pierde. Yes... It's Robert. Isabella will need a little extra time. I have some errands I need her to run. Please allow two hours," I commanded.

"Okay Mr. Elliot. Say no more," Piedre said quickly.

"Great. Thank you." I extended my arms out wide. "See? Now come and spend some time with me. Join me for room service. You work hard all day. Long hours, yes?" I asked her with minimal interest.

"You are so sweet. Yes, I do. I have no choice," she said sadly.

"Hmm. Tell me about it, maybe I can help," I said as I patted the bed next to me. I ran my fingers through her glossy chocolate hair as her big brown eyes gazed back at me on the bed. My eyes roamed to her large breasts straining to be let loose from her maid's outfit.

She moistened her full lips as they lifted into a small smile. "I live in Alentejo with my familia. I have two brothers and one sister. My father is a farmer and we have drought.

Bad drought. He sent me here to work. He said I must provide for the familia. I'm happy here, I like my boss and he treat me well. But I have no choice for the job, because I have to bring money back."

I studied her carefully. A naïve and very beautiful country girl, I slid my hand down her leg... the test. She didn't pull away. She placed her warm fingers over the top of mine. She must have worn her gloves religiously as her hands were in good condition. I brought her hand up to my mouth, kissing and sucking it.

"Do you have a boyfriend?" I breathed in her ear.

"Yes. He's from the same town," she said. I moved her long locks aside as she bit her lip once more. My erection threatened to burst free from my pants as her eyes hungrily watched the growth. I wanted to bend her head to it but let her make the move.

"What he doesn't know won't hurt him." Her cocoa butter scent made me kiss the side of her neck as she moaned joyfully, closing her soft brown eyes. She kneaded my erection through my pants as I released a guttural moan.

"That's it – keep going. You're like a yummy caramel coffee," I breathed into her hair. I liked the slow torture of her caress. I was a man used to getting everything I wanted so I could take my time. I enjoyed the contrast. It would be a crime in itself not to use this full queen size bed with Egyptian cotton sheets to its fullest capacity.

"Mmmm," she murmured as she faced me. I took slow possession over her full bee-stung lips, pulling her bottom lip down with my teeth. I danced over her lips, opening her mouth to play with her tongue. She compiled, matching my passion. Two seconds later she was on my lap with her hands splayed across my broad chest. Without warning Sara's face flashed in front of me with a message.

"But I thought you only wanted me? I thought you were done with them and chasing me?"

The maid continued to kiss me, and for some reason I froze. Even if I thought of another woman while fucking one it didn't stop me. That vision stopped me in mid foreplay. The woman was haunting me from across the waters as my cock started to feel the effects.

"What's wrong, Papi? Is it not good for you?" The sweet sensual young woman on my lap said. She started to grind in frustration.

"No, it's not you. Keep going." I willed myself to push past the invasive vision.

"Okay, just tell me what you like. I'll do it." A keen one, too. I returned to kissing her lips. My next move was to let her zipper down and release the delectable body she had underneath, but my mind wouldn't let me. Ms. Clemens had a hold on me. The parties. Her face. Her body. Her soul, I wanted to possess it. *Fuck.* I pushed the maid off me abruptly to the side.

"Sorry honey. I got some other things on my mind." Shocked, she looked at me, wide-eyed in disbelief and anger.

"Are you serious? You can't finish? But I felt it?" She was standing now pointing to my semi erect cock.

"I know. But my mind is somewhere else. Another time," I said coldly.

"Why not now? I want to..." She pouted. She stepped forward to me and unzipped the back of her maid's uniform. Her voluptuous yet delicate body was shaped like an hourglass just as I imagined.

"I knew that's what you had under the uniform. *I knew it.* But I can't. You can stay here for the next hour," I said, mad at myself. She stood pouting with her hands crossed over her ample breasts, her hair hanging in front of her. My guilt made me walk to my safe.

"Turn around Mami," I demanded.

"Ok. I don't know why you won't sleep with me. I have with others in the hotel. I have experience."

I turned to look at her face, her liquid eyes shone bright waiting for me to change my mind. I retrieved a thick stack of cash from my safe and threw it to her.

"That's for you and your family."

She blinked her eyes rapidly at me. "But we did nothing?" Her ravenous eyes scanned my athletic body.

"I'm a generous man when I want to be." Her pouting turned to a smile as she counted the bills.

"This is too much," she cried as tears ran down her eyes. "You would give me this much?"

"Yes. It's nothing for me. 100,000 dollars." I put my hands in my pockets and looked hard at her, my cock deflated even as I looked at her curvaceous body in front of me.

"How much do the other men pay you? Is that why you like your boss?" I asked with curiosity.

She dropped her head and started crying. "I did it for my family. They don't pay much. I only did it a couple of times." I heard the shame in her voice as she wiped away the tears from her gorgeous face.

My jaw tightened at the news. "If you need more, come and see me. Stop doing it. You're too young and pretty for that. You're not a whore. Remember what I said. I suggest you only give your family a little bit. Keep the rest for yourself. Go on with your life. Start again," I prompted.

"Thank you. Thank you so much." She leaned into me, squashing her boobs against my bare chest as I hugged her back, kissing her shoulder. Her lip trembled as large fat tears rolled to the marbled floor.

"Don't thank me. I was about to fuck you as well." I arched my brow at her and tapped her lightly on the butt, kissing her neck one last time.

"You're a good man." She dressed and looked back at me with her big soft eyes.

"Trust me. I'm not. You just caught me on a good day," I explained. I gave her a thin smile that didn't reach my eyes as she quietly dressed and left the villa. I breathed out a huge sigh when she left. I ran my hands through my dark hair.

What had I become? An obsessed billionaire with the hots for a private investigator who despised me.

Now I couldn't even fuck the help.

5

HAWK

♟

"How'd the shoot go?" I asked Evana.

"Good, baby. Great photographer and cool concept for an editorial shoot. We slayed it."

I heard her click her fingers together and laughed. "How are you, baby?"

I was in Istanbul where East collides with West, a world of mosques, bazaars, grand mystery, colors, spices and gun trafficking at its finest. I was here for the latter and my girl was in Paris.

"I didn't fancy being on stakeout all day, but them's the breaks."

"Catch them yet?" Evana asked impatiently.

"Babe. I'm good, but not *that* good," I responded. My eyes were peeled on a terrace rooftop of one of the most exquisite and famous mosques - the Rustem Pasha Mosque, a holy site to behold with intricate architecture covered with colorful iznik tiles in red and blue. Three men walked into the mosque, except I suspected it wasn't being used for mosque purposes by them. A good diversion tactic on their behalf as a sea of people flowed in and out. The spice bazaar sat right underneath the mosque. One of the group looked to be of Arabic descent, he was robed in all white with traditional headdress. An African man in a golden robe I recognized to be King Abodowie from Tanzania. A malevolent, bloodthirsty gun runner with a stronghold on his country. They greeted one another at the entrance by bowing. The third man was a head shorter than the other two. He, too, possessed an olive skin tone. He appeared to be of Arabic descent, robed in white. He swiveled around, passing a package to the first Arab man as they entered. Interesting. My mark was the first Arab man. Prince Saeed Kabal. A killer of many innocent people and international arms trade dealer to three separate national armies. The US government wanted him stopped, for obvious reasons.

"Hmm. I know. From Paris to Istanbul with an assassin; who would have thought?" Evana quipped. "Homeland Security?"

"Yes, my favorite. Can't talk long but see you tonight. On Facetime anyway. Love you," I said with tenderness I only showed to her.

"Love you too, kick some ass," she said smoothly.

Evana with her porcelain gazelle-like features had long stopped saying "be careful." Now she just told me to kick some ass. I shook my head as I shoved my phone back in my pocket. We decided to make it work - my supermodel Russian girlfriend knew everything now. My mind drifted every so often to the consequences. I had someone else to protect in my life, a reason to stay alive. Besides my parents, who missed me. They knew I worked on highly classified missions, but I spared them the extent. I remembered our last conversation fondly.

"Son, we haven't seen you in over a year. You travel so much. When are you going to come see your poor mother and father?" my mother begged.

"I'll be there soon, I'm on assignment right now in Istanbul." I left out the important details.

"What's the assignment, dear?" my mother asked in curiosity.

"Oh, I just have to retrieve some documents and articles that belong to the United States." No lies - the articles were a dead body and the documents were the emails of the trafficking deals and countries involved. A little fabrication never hurt anyone, especially if it spared a heart attack.

Evana, on the other hand, knew almost everything. I diverted my attention back to the scene. All of my senses were on high alert. Aromatic spices filled the air, voices bartering and heckling for position in the spice bazaar below us, however faint. The crowd had thinned out here. Fewer people. The haunting call to prayer assailed my eardrums from the mosque. With my Native American features, I blended in well along with my prayer cap, turquoise blue polo, sandals and culottes. I moved effortlessly with the crowd, keeping my eye on the golden robe. It was the color that stood out the most.

Worlds of color and a cultural mixing pot existed here. I walked into the mosque bowing my head watching the men. In the main room men bowed and worshipped in front of the minaret. The three passed this room, walking up a spiral staircase on the side of the mosque. I followed several paces behind. I didn't have the luxury of a crowd covering here. My heart rate remained steady as I slipped into the winding staircase. The men's voices echoed off the stone walls. In my pocket I pressed the recorder so I could translate later.

All of them were speaking in their mother tongue of Arabic. A door squeaked open at the top of the stairs. I stole a look out of the small arched windows. Pigeons perched near the top beat their wings flying out of sight from the building. All of the terrace rooftops and remarkable classical buildings that encapsulated the city were visible. As I heard the door shut behind them, I crawled to the top of the step, waiting near the door. Another man was already inside the hidden alcove talking with them. He spoke in English.

"My brother, Miguel Herrera, we are pleased to welcome you to our city. We have some business I see," Prince Saeed spoke.

"Yes, an expansion to the American waters. Reselling back to the stupid Americans. I think I have one to help us," he said clearly. All four of their echoes of wicked laughter bounced off the walls.

"Who might that be?" They asked.

"A billionaire by the name of Robert Elliot. He knows nothing," added Miguel.

WELL I'LL BE DAMNED...

6

SARA

♟

J FK to Dublin, Dublin to Lisbon. I rechecked my ticket, rechecked my nerves and checked the weight of my suitcase one last time. I'd called Dermas after my paranoia in the morning.

"Hi Sara," he answered professionally. I'd rang him early, 6 a.m. on the dot. It was Homeland Security, I expected he was on the clock at all times. Besides, my nerves were on 100 and I was due to fly out.

"Hey Dermas, I know it's early, but I want to have your team check something for me."

"Sure, what can we do for you?" he asked.

"I think someone might have been here last night. I know you're not casing my place anymore…. but my bedroom window has a mark I missed. I took a photo and I wondered if you could match it with your files when you visited from last time. First step," I asked with anxiety.

"Hmm. Okay. I trust your judgement. What made you think something changed?" Dermas asked.

"I heard a noise out front. I thought nothing of it; turned

out to be my neighbor's cat, Meckles. I went to sleep with my light on and I woke up to my light being off hours later and a chip in the bedroom window I didn't see before. I dusted the window. Can you check the results if I can get it to your forensics team?"

"We've cleaned up the Jersey Unit. I have someone in there I trust. But I'm in the area and can pick it up personally if you like and drop it to them," he offered sweetly. I liked the sound of Dermas voice.

"You would do that?" I exclaimed.

"Yes. I'm not far. I have meetings on deck all morning. No skin off my nose. I fly back to Washington tomorrow. Easily done," he said coolly.

"Okay. I don't know how to get it to you. That's the problem. I paid a lot of money for my vacation and I fly out this afternoon."

"Great timing. I can be in Jersey in an hour. I have your address," Dermas cut to the chase.

"Of course, you do," I said slowly. Why the hell was he so eager? Dermas laughed heartily.

"You've been through a lot. I can understand your nervousness. This is a big deal. These are the small details that can be the case breakers, so let's get it cleared up. Hold that photo and I'll get a look at it. I'm going to need a coffee when I get there. Got a coffee spot?"

"Sure do. Best in the neighborhood," I added proudly with more relaxation in my voice.

"Great, Sara – look forward to seeing you, not on the screen," his voice dropped an octave with a hint of flirtiness to it. Blink and you would miss the inflection. But I didn't. I frowned at my phone like it had grown ears.

"Err... Thanks," I answered awkwardly. I guessed I would find out the flirt vibe in an hour. I looked around the place and it looked like a bombshell hit it. I looked at my criminal wall and it still had Elliot's face all over it. A spark of hot electric current hit the pit of my stomach as I stared at his face. I swallowed down the guilty lump in my throat. If anybody knew that I'd kissed him I would be called in for questioning. That was a given. The cryptic note he left I packed in my suitcase. I wasn't risking Dermas and his team finding it. A crucial piece of evidence so close to the mark. There was really no rhyme or reason why I kept it in my possession.

Why did I have it?

Why didn't I just hand it over?

Let them trace the ink from the page...

In my heart I knew why, but I didn't want to admit to myself. As I turned the letter over in my hands staring at myself in the mirror, I knew I wanted Elliot to find me. I wanted him to access me. That deviant little imp wanted to find out what the unfinished business would be between us.

The hour came up quick and Dermas showed up with a three-peat rap of the knuckles on my door. I double- taked with a sharp intake of air when he arrived, because in front of me was a very handsome man. Not at all what I expected. On the call from the last case maybe I was too involved to see it, but this man was classically good looking and well built. Early forties, with symmetrical features, shaved head, milk chocolate, a warm inviting smile and caramel eyes.

As soon as I opened the door my stomach settled. I'm sure he had a wife and kids at home, so my look of admiration didn't last too long.

"Hi Sara, all packed and ready to go I see." Derma stood in the door frame pointing to my suitcase.

"Yep. And not a moment too soon. Come on in," I gestured.

Dermas with his hands in his taupe pants pockets floated straight to the criminal board. "Still got it up, I see. No wonder you're stressed out. Gotta look at this shitbag all day. This guy's a tough cookie and he's so heavily cloaked it's like trying to find a needle in a haystack."

I frowned with dispirited resignation. "I hear what you're saying. I want to nail this sucker to the wall, though." I gritted through my teeth. The small detail that I left out was I *literally* wanted Elliot to nail me to the wall and take possession over my undersexed body. But I would skip that part.

Derma scouted his eyes over the place, looking around. "Let me take a look at the photo and the window. That'll let me know whether I need to get the New Jersey team in here to do a sweep."

"Ok, come on through." I led Dermas to my bedroom window and placed my face close to where the timber was split in the far-right corner. Dermas put his face close to mine and I swallowed hard from his warm breath next to my face. His penetrating gaze was concentrated on the timber split.

"Let me bring the photos from the forensic team up so I can see." Dermas brought out his phone and held it to the window frame. He flinched a little. "Hard to say, not much in it." He turned sideways to gauge my reaction. The tension in my body was evident. "I'll get a team in here to do a sweep, though. Just in case. You cool with that?" he asked, watching my face.

I grimaced a little. I really wanted to be present when they did the sweep. "How about we wait 'til I get back? I have an alarm system anyway and a lot of nosey neighbors. I'm sure everything will be fine." I flashed him a withdrawn smile. A little tingle in my spine told me something else, but I ignored it.

"We can do that. Now, how about that coffee? When Dermas smiled, I realized how beautiful his teeth were. Just like Elliot's. He was a nice height at six feet tall. Not too tall and not too short. I grabbed my bag and my keys, happy to be in his company.

"Don't mind walking?" I asked in a challenging tone. I expected him to say yes.

"No, lead the way." Very charming man. I bobbed my head in appreciation.

"So Sara, you been here a while?" Dermas casual easy stroll made me feel at ease.

"Yes. I've been in this house for a few years now. I love living here. It doesn't have the hustle and bustle of New York, but I still love the village feel. Everybody looks out for one another."

"Good to be out of the city, huh?" he agreed.

"Yes, I lived there for a little while when I was younger. I thought I was going to make it big as a photographer, taking the world by storm," I said dreamily. "But now look. I'm a small-time investigator from Maywood, New Jersey."

Dermas arched his eyebrow at me. "Small time? You've helped us break open the vault to one of the most notorious billionaires in New York. That's not a small-time thing, by any means."

I chuckled a little. We passed Mrs. Darcy who was out on her stoop as always. Her rollers were in and she couldn't give a damn. Her sharp eyes gave me a look of wariness. We had an understanding since she sent some goons packing on my behalf.

"Morning, Mrs. Darcy," I called out. I gave her an overhead wave with my left hand.

She smiled back, pretending to water her geraniums at the front. "Morning Sara, *and* friend."

"Good Morning to you," Dermas smiled at her politely. I'm sure I saw Mrs. Darcy's face flush red, blushing from his charm.

We kept strolling and I felt a little awkward. I'd let go of the guy I'd given my number to Little Birdy. He hadn't called, so I had no reason to care about bringing Dermas there. Little Birdy café had its usual buzz going on. A hipster girl with a short fringe and long hair was talking animatedly to another brunette with a long dress. A line of three people was in front of us, as it wasn't peak hour. Little Birdy usually slowed down mid-morning. The coffee machine was in full swing as I watched the steam float out of the machine. Local artists had their artwork hanging around the place, beautiful illustrated versions of little birds. Fresh little flowers were on each table. Josie, one of the long-time waitresses moved past me with a plate of eggs, avocado and bacon on sourdough toast. Made my mouth water.

"Hey Sara. We missed you, haven't seen you in a couple of days," she said on the whizz by.

"I know I've been busy," I lied. I didn't want to run into Devin and his questions.

I could feel Dermas's gaze on me. "I'm impressed. This is a nice place. I like their teal walls, real funky. This is your regular, I'm guessing?" he asked.

"Yep, it's my favorite spot."

"I can see why. My shout. Those eggs looked really good. Making me hungry."

I laughed. "Yep there's always something good to eat here."

I stepped up to the counter. Behind it there was no sign of Devin. I breathed a sigh of relief. I ordered my usual coffee, moving to the side so Dermas could order. I spotted a window seat which I loved and silently moved to the seat.

"Good choice. I like to read what's on the walls of cafés. I'm going to check this out." He said. I watched as Dermas spotted a newspaper article encased in plexiglass on the wall. I frowned. I didn't see it here last time. The title at the top of the wall was dubbed *'The Locals'*

"Let me see. I've never seen that before," I swung out of my seat to look at the wall with Dermas. On it was a local red-headed musician who I recognized to be part of a mainstream band along with an article about the coffee he liked to drink. Brought a smile to my face. Then underneath was a local biologist and what coffee they drank. Next to it made my mouth fall open as an audible gasp sprang from my lips. An article which I did for publicity after the last case. *Photographer turned private investigator. Sara Clemens.* There I was in my crimson red jacket standing near the Keansburg Fishing pier, on a foggy morning. I distinctly remember the photographer saying to me before the photos, *"We want there to be an air of mystery about you. So, if we meet at the pier early in the morning we should get a nice foggy atmospheric shot."*

I felt my cheeks overheating with embarrassment. "I cannot believe they put this up here," I said under my breath. I looked around at the alleged culprits at the counter.

Dermas threw his two cents in. "Local town hero it is. You're famous," his brown eyes teased.

"That's why I have to get out of here a while," I said in an annoyed voice. My stomach turned a few times as I thought about the media exposure; it triggered bad memories of that slimy alien-like chameleon - the Viper- who was still out there. I closed my eyes briefly reopening them with Dermas eyes fastened on me.

"It's a good thing. Will bring you more business." I paused a beat before speaking. That's what I was supposed to feel, but I didn't. I just wanted to hide. "Has it?" he queried.

"Yes and no. Smaller jobs which I have, but I'm happy about that. I want a break from this madness. I was in the headlines for over a week. My mother called me nonstop for two weeks after that," I added with exasperation.

Dermas glanced at me. "Yikes. That bad, huh? Come on, let's sit down, our coffees are here."

Josie with her effervescent smile came over and ceremoniously placed our coffees on the table. She nodded in the direction of the wall. "Ah, you saw it. You made the cut," she winked.

"Yes. I saw it," I said simply, a chaste smile on my lips.

Derma slid in his chair and I mine. I lifted the steaming brew of caffeinated goodness to my lips.

"You mentioned your parents. Do they live around here?" He asked with keen interest.

"Yep. Not far. Feels far, though, because I haven't seen them in a while," I observed.

Dermas took a sip of his coffee. "I know the feeling. That reminds me that I have to call my mother. She's turning 74 in a couple of weeks."

I arched an eyebrow at Dermas. "I hope I make it to that age."

"You and me both," he chuckled with a dimple showing up that made him more appealing.

"Where are your parents from originally?" he asked.

"My father is from the islands, Tortola and my mother is a New Jersey Native," I explained.

Derma locked his cute brown eyes on me. "Wow. That's quite a mix."

"It's a good one. I've been to the islands a couple of times. Good people."

"I bet. You got anyone special in New Jersey?" he asked quickly, moving on from the subject.

"No. Just working my cases and trying to build up my case portfolio. I'm glad to have a break from it, though."

"That's good," his eyes lingered on me a little longer than they should.

"We might have a little information about Elliot and his whereabouts but I'm waiting on a lead to confirm." Derma's tone was pensive.

"Okay. Can you give me the vicinity?" My interest piqued, I blew over my coffee and Dermas smiled a little too hard. The guy was married, but judging by the heat coming to my cheeks he was interested.

"He's definitely out of the country. There are some trans-actions we're trying to trace right now. They are European based," Dermas confirmed.

"Europe. No more specific than that?" I asked in tempered frustration.

"No, unfortunately. We'll have to wait and see what his movements look like." Dermas looked at his watch. "What time do you leave for the airport?"

"I'm leaving here at 1 for a 5 p.m. flight. That way I touch down in Portugal early morning and don't lose a day," I beamed as I let the excitement sink in.

Dermas nodded. "Nice. I'm separated by the way," he tapped his fingers on his coffee cup. *Ah – now I see. Shooting your shot.* "Maybe when you get back, I could take you out on a date when I'm down this way next." Dermas smiled and I pressed my legs together. Apparently, it was raining men in New Jersey.

"How separated are you?" I responded, scanning him. Seemed like a nice clean-cut guy, but I for one knew how deceiving looks could be.

Dermas reached across the table and put his warm hand over the top of mine. I didn't move my hands; I wasn't 100% for some reason about him. "The divorce papers are being served as we speak. I wish I could stay and talk to you more but I gotta make it back on this Washington run," he added.

"Running the gauntlet?" I quipped, grateful for the change in conversation. He missed the fact I didn't answer his date question.

"Yep. Say hi to Hawk when you see him next," he flashed a bright smile at me.

"I will. Walk back?" I said.

"Well my car's parked at your place, unless you got a magic carpet." We laughed together.

"Of course, I was elsewhere, just anxious about the trip," I confessed as I dropped a tip on the table.

"I get it, but it will be fine, you'll forget about it when you touch down."

I peered around the lunch crowd streaming in. None other

than the absentee caller Devin had now slipped behind the coffee machine. My stomach felt queasy and I wanted to leave. I had nothing to say to him. I regretted the fact I gave him my number. Call it a moment of weakness or 'meh' something like that. In my mind I was trying to get my dating hours up. I shrunk down beside Dermas as we strolled out of the door. When I looked up I saw the disappointed eyes of the barista. I said nothing. Dermas put his hand in the small of my back as he led me out of the door.

"Everything ok?" He shot me a puzzled look as we stepped outside.

"Yup. Fine, why?"

"I don't know... Were you avoiding someone?" Dermas gave me a suspicious look.

"Should have known – you're Homeland Security after all."

"Yep. You can't slide much past me. The barista guy?" Derma's voice went up a notch in pitch.

"*Well,*" I threw my hands up as the cool of the New Jersey air hit my lungs. "Well, just a misplaced fan, I think. I didn't feel like talking to him."

We reached my house pretty quickly, with Dermas's Jeep waiting in the driveway.

"Understandable. I'm a fan too. Just in a different way." He said quietly with his brown eyes staring back at me.

"Thanks. I think." Dermas dimples made another appearance as he tapped the top of his car.

"Alright, Ms. Clemens, enjoy your trip. Stay safe and call me if you hear anything and I'll do the same."

"Thanks for coming all the way out," I said, appreciative of his efforts.

"Pleasure's all mine. See you, Sara." He waved and placed his well-formed physique into the driver's seat of his car.

♟

THE BACK of the Uber was clean and neat, the driver had the radio on low. The traffic was New York usual. Heavy, congested and annoying. I was happy about my trip as I let the tension in my overworked body go. I vowed to let the stresses of Elliot's case not get in the way of a good time. I laid my head back on the seat resting my eyes. The tiredness and intense adrenaline from being fixated on one central human for the last few months had taken its toll. I couldn't wait to arrive in Portugal to my villa. I tapped my feet a little with hope.

I was keeping it casual and comfortable for the flight. Jeans, a tee, my vans and a light jacket for when they pumped up the air conditioning on the plane.

As we arrived at the airport, I felt the peaking excitement bubbling up in my stomach. All I wanted was to board that plane. To get the hell out of the United States for a while.

"Thanks," I said as my courteous Uber driver popped the trunk and I got out.

People were lined up outside the entrance of the airport, offloading their bags like me and kissing their loved ones. I'd called my mother last minute to tell her. I smirked as I thought about her reaction.

"You're going where? When? Do you need a ride to the airport?" I listened as the queen of fretting began her tirade.

"No, Ma. I'm good. I just need a culture change for a little while. Spread my wings," I advised. My mother was a planned person so things not part of the schedule threw her off.

"Well okay, you do need a break. Have fun over there and be safe. Who are you flying with, I need to check the crash rates..."

"*Ma!* Stop. It will be fine. I chase bad guys for a living, remember?"

I could feel her fanning her face from the airport. "Don't remind me."

"Ma, I gotta go, give Daddy a kiss for me," I said, getting her off the phone.

"I will. Love you."

"Love you, too, bye."

I let the Uber driver pull my large duffle bag out of the trunk. I wanted to dance around. This was my first time in such a long time going on a trip.

"Alright now, have a good trip, Ms. Clemens," the driver said.

"Thank you. I will," I beamed, wanting to squeal.

I breezed in through the airport doors, checked in through international customs and kept myself occupied until take off. My phone pinged just before.

Have a great trip! Hawk.

Portugal, here I come. I texted him back with a smile.

Strangely enough the nooks and crannies of my mind continuously circled back to Elliot. Time and time again. The kiss that rocked my world. Some sort of connection that I'd never experienced before. Maybe we knew each other from past lives. Who knows? But his energy spoke to mine in such a primal way it scared me. The memory caused me to shudder with desire as I waited at the airport lounge. I gulped him away. I would be in Lisbon, Portugal soon enough.

Most of the plane ride I amused myself with the movies, enjoying my half a cup of orange juice and not a half bad airplane meal. By the time I landed in Portugal my patience for being on a winged aircraft was worn thin.

Lisbon Portele Airport, a standard airport experience. The time being 7 a.m. Lisbon time. I headed to the nearest toilet to splash some water on my face and come alive before I picked up my bags from the carousel. I rolled on some deodorant, brushed my teeth and bounced along to grab my bags. Travelers from all around the world were in the airport. Some rushing, some strolling to their chosen destinations. I was in stroll mode. I retrieved my bags and checked my phone with the hotel reservation information. Almada, twenty minutes give or take from Lisbon. I wanted a different experience from the normal tourist, so I decided to stay just outside of the mix and across the Tagus River. Once outside, I put my hand up to hail down a taxi. A large white sedan pulled up.

"Oi como você está" The slightly built Portuguese driver said.

"Boa," I replied, meaning good. He'd asked me how I was, he seemed impressed that I knew that. I knew the basics. I cringed, hoping I would be able to speak English. I had Google translate on my phone so I felt okay. I pulled my phone out of my pocket; it was fully charged. I breathed a sigh, that's the last thing I wanted to happen. "English?" I ventured.

"Madam, I speak perfect English. I thought I would indulge you. I'm Donovan. Where can I take you today?" he asked brightly. Phew.

"Umm... I'm staying in Almada. A villa there," I looked nervously at my notebook with the address.

Donovan moved my bag to the trunk, grinning. "Ah, Almada. Interesting. Most want to stay in the action of Lisbon. Almada is a fine choice. Right near the waterfront and over the bridge." He pointed in the direction of the destination.

"Yes. I thought I might try something adventurous," I smiled. *Now* I felt like I was on holiday. The air smelt different here. Fresh, crisp and with a touch of European mugginess.

I slid inside the taxi as Donovan, the dark-haired man said; "If you want adventure, I can be a tour guide for the week. I will give you my card. I will take you to some little-known places here and it will blow your mind." Donavan's accent and affable nature was charming to me. I shook my head in hesitation as I thought it through. I didn't reply.

As we drove, I admired the new scenery and the landscape of a new city. For the first time in months I felt more relaxed than I ever had. I vowed to think about nothing to do with the case. *Absolutely nothing.* I wanted to create a void where new memories of Portugal could fall in.

Donavan peered at me in the rear view mirror. "We are about to travel over the de Abril Bridge, this is the only bridge that connects Lisbon to Almada. Used to be an industrial area, you know. Lots of locals and some tourists come over on the ferry from Lisbon.

"Ah, I hope to meet them. I'm loving it already," I said excitedly.

We rode over the towering suspension bridge that connected Lisbon to Almada as I felt the weight of it underneath us, reminding me of San Francisco.

"Did you think any more of my offer?" he asked, peering at me in the mirror.

"I prefer to find my own way, but I will call you for pick-ups. Is that okay?"

Donavan saluted from the front. "Perfecto! If you want to go on a day trip call me first and I can tell you if it's good to go or a rip off. 'Kay?"

"Awesome." I looked out at the huge expanse known as the Tagus River as we crossed the bridge. I had a great view of the whole shore of Portugal. It was overrun with terracotta roof terraces and green rolling hills in the background. A breathtaking sight to behold. I was still in awe that I wasn't in the United States anymore – that was enough for me.

"What is the villa called that you stay at?" Donavan asked.

I fumbled around in my purse. I had the address scribbled down on a piece of lined paper.

"One minute…" I scraped it up from the bottom of my bag, reading it out. "Casa la Rosa."

"Ah yes, very nice Madam. You pick well, sophisticated taste. The villa used to be owned by a distasteful character in the 1980's. Then he sold it."

"Really? Distasteful?" I leaned forward; I was staying in an intriguing villa. Now I was really excited. "Tell me more."

Donovan laughed. I liked him – he had a calm, sweet disposition. He would make a great tour guide.

"Yes, a ruthless drug kingpin. He owned the ports here, too. He's dead now. Lived until his late 70's. His name was Alcendro Carleon. The guy killed thousands in his lifetime, but helped some others, too," Donovan shrugged and poked out his lip.

"I didn't read any of this anywhere," I frowned.

"Ah – and you won't. That's the beauty of us locals. We know what's real and what is not. It's not spoken of as they've tried to clean up the image of Portugal. We have the decriminalization of drugs, so things are much better now. We have a low crime rate and a very peaceful existence. Not like Columbia." Donavan slowed down and circled into the driveway of the villas. The reception was a faint lemon-yellow building with terracotta roofs and arched windows. Palm trees swayed lightly in the breeze around the luxurious villa.

The sound of splashing rang in my ears. It was coming from the right, where a pool existed. Donovan came to a stop right out front, handing me his card.

"Madam, Clemens. Here you go. Please call. This side has some of the best views of Lisbon, if not with me be sure to see our national icon the Santuário de Cristo Rei. It's right here in Almada."

"I noticed that. Amazing, and I can't wait to see it."

I opened my door up as Donovan got out to collect my bags from the trunk. I slid my sunglasses down onto my face, jumping out of the taxi, ready for where Portugal wanted to take me. Donovan handed me my large duffel bag and I grabbed it with two hands.

"Thank you, Donovan. I will be in touch."

"Please. Enjoy your experience in Portugal." His big smile took up most of his face.

"Oh, I plan to." Donovan started his engine and moved off from the curb. The pool looked extremely inviting. I merely glanced, but that was long enough. A well-toned athletic figure emerged from the water, making my blood curdle. My head began to pound with overwhelming intensity. I struggled to keep my bag from slipping from my hands. My fingers unfurled slowly; my feet kept me cemented to the spot. My mouth became a bundle of cotton, with no reprieve for moisture. I was like a camel in the desert, thirsting. My hands trembled from the adrenaline coursing through my weak veins.

Danger. Danger.

No. Please no. I beg you.

Couldn't be.

I felt my womb tighten with sickening desire. My stomach bundling into wicked knots. Sensations I tried to run from all these months were hitting me with brute force in one moment. The finely-honed man glided like silk to collect his towel on the side of the pool. Wiping the glistening beads of water from his tanned skin and over his slick dark hair, he wiped his delicious body down. He hadn't seen me yet. My feet felt like lead, still rooted to the spot. I was staring into the mouth of a beautiful devil, a few seconds from being caught. From across the waters and a million of miles away there stood Robert Elliot in all his glory.

7

HAWK

I grimaced in the shadows. Elliot was everywhere, his tentacles were long, his tainted hands running through numerous dirty international networks. I stilled my whisper-like breath. I'd trained to drop my heart rate to 28 bpm, part of my army practice and with my native ancestors. I clicked on my listening device to record their conversation.

"We will tie in the shipments together with Elliot's and reach new customers right under the US government's nose. I will make the necessary arrangements," Miguel explained.

"I trust you will be able to convince this billionaire you speak of?" Prince Saeed replied, sounding hesitant.

"He will have no choice. He needs treaty protection and my port operations to expand his empire. He will just be adding a new product. Shouldn't bother him." Miguel's textured dirty laugh rang out through the small cove. King Abodowie shook the slight man's hand and the Arabs, who bowed to him.

"We are now officially partners. When will the first shipment leave Portuguese ports?"

"In the next month, continue your shipment to me and they will be housed until we can move. All the necessary officials have been notified of the arrangement," Miguel added.

The Arabs laughed. "We are set to rule the world and make a lot of money. We cannot be stopped." All three death traders laughed at their cunning, but flawed plans.

"Come, let us go now. Let's break bread. We'll return for another meeting at the mosque the next day to seal the deal," Prince Saeed commanded. I sucked in hard oxygen as they moved. My main objective was to chop off the head of the operation and to track the shipping to discover the networks and report back to US Homeland Security.

On the other side of the room, I noted an exit. They moved towards it. I waited until I heard the click of the door locking on my side. Pigeon wings flapped overhead distracting me for a moment. I could hear movement from downstairs in the mosque as those at worship set off back to work. I slid down the door to peek between the wide cracks of light. Two pairs of feet opening the other door to the outside. I painstakingly inched the door open from my side. No need for my lock-picking kit. I moved feather light to the shadows of the small room, swiftly gliding to the door they'd just exited. Three men with echoing footsteps moved down a winding staircase, speaking in Arabic. I fastened my gaze on them as they reached the bottom of the geometrically tiled staircase.

The oxygen rushed into my lungs as my beats per minute rose to normal level. I followed them with patience through the bazaar with its high arched dome. The calm banter of customers and retailers talking, haggling and conversing sounded like background noise to me. Retailers selling vibrant aromatic spices by the bag stood out front of their stalls waiting for potential customers. All shades of the earth, ranging from canary yellow cumin to deep rust colored turmeric existed. Small red Turkish flags hung from the taupe brick in between every stall. Trinkets displaying the country were displayed on small free-standing stalls. It reminded me to grab a souvenir for Evana. Belts, t-shirts, shoes, head-scarves and intricately patterned hookahs were being sold in abundance. Turkish delight in huge mounds in varying colors took whole quarters of the bazaar. Lentils and grains of all assortments filtered through my eyes. I never lost sight of the men as they headed out of the bazaar, however. Out front, the trio packed into a sleek black limousine. A white taxi flew by and I flagged it down, tapping the top. The driver skidded to a halt.

"Where you go?" The driver said in an irritated voice.

"Follow that black limousine," I said sternly.

"I cannot."

"Yes, you can," I handed him a roll of American dollars. "Wherever they go, you go."

"Of course, of course." He quickly changed his tune. The car weaved delicately around the Istanbul traffic. A sea of people surrounded the area, swarming it in fact, like bees to a honeypot. The vehicle stopped at a large outdoor shopping square. "Thanks," I said abruptly as I exited.

I watched as Prince Saeed moved through the crowd with swiftness and into the heart of the paved eating area. The other two followed. I wanted to see where they were going. I needed to exchange a little gift with him. I'd thrown my prayer cap in the trash as I walked. I unbuttoned my shirt and off loaded it, revealing a loose white t-shirt. The key was to continue blending in with the busy Istanbul crowd. More markets and heavy aromatics invaded my senses. I picked up pace, placing a small tracking device in my hand which once opened released particles which adhered to the hair follicles of the person close by. Those microscopic particles would allow me to track the Prince through thermal heat sensing. I pretended to see a friend along the path where people were hustling and bustling. I looked dead ahead. I pushed past the Prince who was wide open on my left-hand side.

"Sorry, sorry," I said as I placed my hands up. We locked eyes and I looked deep into the cold-blooded eyes of a high-profile killer. He said nothing and returned to talking with the other two men. Part one complete.

I watched the three men move up the stairs of one of the brown stone buildings. I mulled around the entrance pretending to pick something up from the ground. I wanted more intel, especially now that I knew Elliot was involved. The terrain was rocky. I'd been told by my superior:

Take him out. They might have someone else to replace him, but take him out. We're sending a message. Then the next one we take out. Any associates connected that you see, get us the names. We'll take it from there.

My mission was crystal clear. All I needed was the right shot with Prince Saeed, alone. Not so easy – the dude after all was a prince, flanked with bodyguards everywhere he went. As I watched the dark figures approach the top of the stairs, I tested the door for creaking. No sound. I deftly squeezed in and flattened myself under the stairwell as I heard them speaking in Arabic. I pressed my tape recorder; I would decipher it later. I smelt the aroma of mouth-watering food up above. They were about to have a feast, that's for sure. No-one was speaking in English, which was a crutch for me. I only knew a Spanish fluently and French. I would need to translate. I crept closer to the heavy wooden doors and pitter pattered to the top of the stairs with ninja-like moves. I placed a small device in the corner of the door, moving to the upper chambers of the stairs, out of visible sight. The listening piece in my ear allowed me to hear their conversation loud and clear.

The conversation switched to English as Miguel chimed in. I wanted to know where he was from. The scraping of chairs pierced my ear drums as they sat down. There must have been another entrance, otherwise how did they get the food up and down the stairs?

Sitting tight I pressed the piece to my ear. Sometimes I really loved my job, and this was one of those days. If I could nail Elliot at the same time it would be a major coup.

"When did you begin the process of working with the American? What proof is there of these ports?" Prince Saeed queried in his rich Arabic accent.

"He owns all of the Ports of New York, ample for our operation. As you know we run our artillery across the Black Sea with Russian carriers. Once those carriers change over to American waters, this will expand not only the cocaine operation but our arms trade operation."

"I see. Tell me: is he trustworthy?" Prince Saeed asked. Silverware dropped on the plate as I heard music play. I noted the third Middle Eastern didn't speak at all.

"He is so far. I'm watching him. His father and mine go back in time. We have dealings. He will do as I say, he is listed with Interpol for questioning in his home country. As long as he complies, we shouldn't have a problem. Portugal is a very forgiving country."

Okay, so Miguel was from Portugal.

"The percentages should remain in our favor, should they not?" King Abodowie's voice boomed aggressively. Static cut in and I pressed the earpiece to my ear harder.

"Yes," Miguel stated.

"Then a great deal has been made. We require an increase in supplies as we are preparing for the invasion into the Congo. We have business there. All of the requirements will be sent to your people," the King boomed again. His voice like rolling thunder. I knew what he wanted those guns for. His militant armies, which pillaged villages rampantly. This was one of his well-known practices as he worked to slowly take over the whole of Central Africa.

Now I had plenty to go on. My hand went to my forehead to wipe the excess sweat from the mucky heat of Istanbul, leaving the scene at 1500 hours. I'd managed to snag accommodation nearby. Pulling my phone out of my pocket I called the US Homeland Security agent check-in line.

"Three peat. Abodowie, another unidentified person, Miguel from Portugal supplying the cover; tracing the voice file and photos upon base return. On target to extinguish in two days. Connected to Robert Elliot. Wanted on Interpol. Location not yet established." I clicked off the phone.

I stepped into the suffocating heat made worse by the number of locals and tourists. I glided into the closest taxi, riding back to my accommodation. My phone rang in the vehicle.

"Hi baby," my spy voice changed to one of tenderness; my lady was on the phone.

"Hey. How was your day?" she asked. Trick question at this point.

"Oh, you know, went to the mosque and the spice bazaar to check out a few things. Do you want something from there?" Code for *I was staking out bad guys in the mosque and chasing them down through the spice bazaar...* now she knew what I meant. Besides, I never spoke to Evana on the cell phone about business.

"Sounds perfect. Will you be done by next week? Ready for me?"

"Yes, I am. I can't wait to see that gorgeous face of yours. I miss you," I dropped the octave of my voice to bedroom sexy as the driver pulled up to Neorion Hotel.

"Talk a little later, honey," I said, finishing up the brief call.

"Bye, sweety," she cooed, exiting the call.

A sandy-color square building with geometric blue tiles stood with black railings. A merging of cultures reflected in one building. I moved hastily to my room. I swiped my electronic hotel card in the door, listening for the click to open. Stripping off my shirt I let the Istanbul air slide over my hot skin as I entered. I loosened my shoulders from the day's tensions, sighing as I bent down to the safe.

"24-18-30," I muttered as I unlocked the safe. I retrieved my listening devices, including recorders and two laptops. I set them up and grabbed the hotel menu. My stomach was rumbling. Looked like I was eating in for the night. The room had a wooden back panel that doubled as a bed post, a large panoramic classical painting of Istanbul above it and most importantly, clean sheets and a place to lay my head.

My mouth watered as I scanned the hotel menu. I opted for the no-brainer: pizza. I took out a cold beer from the fridge.

My phone rang. An international call, I peered closer at the number. Sara. Boy, did I have news for her.

"Hi. How you doing? Doing it tough in Portugal?" I queried.

"Hawk. I have to tell you something." The eeriness in her voice made my senses prick up as the whooshing sound from popping the beer tab let out.

"Sounds juicy. Tell me," I said.

"Hawk. *Elliot's here.*" I let out a dry chuckle. "What's funny? What the hell? I'm going-"

I drained a third of my beer before answering. A long day and the cold alcoholic liquid felt good sliding down my throat. "What's funny is I knew. *Sort of.* You just gave me a little more of the puzzle. Let me explain, then we can work out a game plan."

"Okayyyy," Sara responded with flustered confusion.

"Elliot is connected to an arms and coke dealer. Guy's name is Miguel. I don't know his surname, but he runs out of Portugal and is going to cover Elliot in terms of extradition. From the sound of the audio I got today the guy has connections. So, he's high up in the ranks."

Sara's' heavy sigh strained through the line. "So even if I get photographic evidence and send it through it doesn't guarantee Interpol is going to work with us?"

"Yes and no. Just have to get the photos in the right hands.

He can't have all of Interpol on lock," I reasoned as I stretched my long muscular legs out.

"Right."

"So, these guys are heavy. Deep doo-doo. International trade for arms trafficking. Miguel is planning on using Elliot to ship into the New York ports," I explained.

"Okay. If I can get a look at the players, I can put together the profiles and send through to Dermas," I literally heard her mind ticking over.

"Right."

"Who is the target?" she asked sharply.

"Hmm. Where you are calling me from?" I hesitated with the answer as I took another mouthful of beer.

"Burner phone. I brought one when I got here. Go ahead," she was eager for the information.

"Good. You're learning fast," I quipped.

"Shuddup, Hawk," she snapped. I didn't mind getting her riled up.

"Alright, alright – hold onto your bikini. Prince Saeed. One of the filthiest rich men on the planet. Huge in the arms dealing game," I finally released.

"Shit. These are major players. That's a tough network to bring down," she gasped.

"That's the thing: *he's* the mark. I've been directed to pick them off one by one. Send a message. They won't know where it's coming from. It will let them know they are being watched. If it can be set up like they're against one another, even better. They might take out one another…"

"Or you could get busted and taken out," she said cautiously. I shook my head. Caution? Against assassin code. We ventured where no man would.

"Oh, ye of little faith. Got my grandfather on my side. Never fails," I calmly replied.

"That you do. Not going to argue with you there," she said softly. I powered up my computers. I wanted to log in and trace Miguel's photo. "I'm going to identify the players. I'll send you the shots," I said, the beer was going down real nice. "Be careful. I got two days 'til the job is done here. I don't know how that will impact how they move," I warned.

"Hard to do that when I'm staying at the same hotel as Elliot." Sara dropped the lethal bombshell with a thickening dose of irony.

"Sheeettttt. Stay out of sight. Don't try anything. Wait 'til I get there Sara," I warned again. Thing is, I knew she wouldn't listen. I knew she would take photos and follow him. My stomach rumbled. I was waiting on that pizza so I could think straight.

"I will. I know he's got the penthouse villa. I'll find out more and keep you posted."

"You're vulnerable. You have no weapons and no allies," I pushed.

"Don't you think I know that?" Sara hissed like a cat back at me. "Give me some credit. Sorry for yelling. I'm just on edge a little," she corrected.

"Understandable. I don't take offense." A knock at the hotel door came. "My pizza's here. Look, let me at least get that name back to you, so you know what you're dealing with. I know you, Sara. You can't help but sniff things out. So, let me get the name. I have associates there; if you get in a situation, I can get you strapped pronto."

"*See*, so I'm not unarmed." Sometimes the woman was impossible. I stretched my long limbs out, opening the door. A nervous-looking porter came with a pizza on a table and wheeled it in. A complimentary beer was on the trolley with it. I smiled, handing the porter a tip of $30US. I watched his mouth twitch into a smile. I had the phone tucked under my ear listening to Sara.

"Okay. You got your camera and binoculars, right?"

"Yes, so to me technically I'm armed, plus my phone and the listening devices you gave me. So I am, in a way, armed."

Sighing deep I ran my hand through my unruly dark hair. It was getting kind of long. Evana liked it though, so I kept it for her. I sat down at my computer and opened it up. I plugged in all the batteries. I kept talking.

"Where are you right now?"

"I'm in my room. Trying to decide what the fuck to do about this crazy situation," she seethed.

"I don't know, this could be of benefit the way I see it. If Elliot wanted to take you out, he would have already done it. He knew where you lived already. The Viper was sent for Evana, you just happened to be in the way," I reiterated in a matter-of-fact tone.

"Don't remind me. Tell her that she owes me big time," Sara added sarcastically.

"She misses you. We can't get together for obvious reasons. So, since you're so hell bent on following Elliot... lemme log into the mainframe and get the photo recognition of this guy. One sec." I typed in my code, putting my finger up to the screen for ID purposes. I pulled up the photo, dragging my finger across the touchscreen to place it where I wanted. I watched the database scroll through faces and names. A familiar clicking sound stopped and my screen beeped at me.

"Anything?" Her impatience got the better of her.

"Yes. Minor drug charge, late 1990's. Nothing since then. Got smart obviously. Connections to the Pistoleros crew. Technically, Elliot is being called for questioning – he's not being accused of murder. The only hope is if Clope snitches. But they can't pin anything on him yet, either. They have circumstantial evidence and no weapon. It's looking like Elliot is a free man. If enough time elapses, things are going to go away like all the other bullshit he's done."

"What about that university hustle case? Is it cold? Why can't it be reopened? Can't we work on that and pick away? That's a case they won't suspect." I heard rustling around.

"*We?* I'm an assassin. I don't have time for digging unless it's for my wedgie. I get what I need and dispose of the mark. Quick and easy." I sewed that option up.

"You're a real ass, you know that?" she threw back at me.

"Probably, but I get the job done. There you go. What happened with Dermas, by the way?"

"Hmmm. I told him to wait 'til I got back. I don't want them sniffing around my apartment while I'm not there," she said warily.

'You afraid they'll find your dildo?" I teased.

"Hardy har. What is with you? He did ask me out, which was creepy to me," Sara confided.

"Hey you're hot. But isn't he married?"

"So, I thought, too... He's separated, which means to me 'I'm still sticking to my wife on occasion.' By the way did you just call me hot?"

"Gotta call it like I see it, honey. I hope you find yourself a nice European while you're there. Loosen up, live a little. Dermas... Hmm I don't know if he's your type. Too clean cut."

"Ugh, you're dishing out love advice now?"

"Hmm, well I got the girl, didn't I? And if I recall I warned you about Elliot... See you in two. Bye." I didn't want to hang on, my pizza was getting cold.

"Bye, Hawk."

8

SARA

E lliot. Here. Now. I shut my eyes and tried to reason with the thumping in my chest but no dice. I hitched my duffel bag over my shoulder further, ducking inside before the untamed specimen clamped eyes on me. A deep frustration inside me burned as to why our attraction ran so deep and true. How is it I wanted to merge with the devil incarnate? I shook my head and moved inside the villa resort. A slim man greeted me at the counter. I usually liked to look around the lobby of a place, but right then I couldn't see anything but fury entwined with desire.

"Hi, I'm Piedre, the manager of Casa La Rosa. Welcome." An olive-skinned man flung his arm up in a grand gesture while I remained tight lipped, scared Elliot would pop out at any minute.

"Errr, thank you. Nice to be here. I made a reservation the other day," straight down to business. I looked around making sure the coast was clear.

"I know, I take care of all the bookings. The American. You look like one of us with that caramel skin," he said with a leery grin. I coughed a little. Piedre was getting a little too close.

"Thanks again. I just want to get my room keys and freshen up."

"Of course, of course," he coaxed. "You have a wonderful villa that overlooks the Tagus. You can see everything from there. Enjoy your stay, take some brochures with you. Ask me anything you need to know. If you want a taxi, I can call one from here and they won't charge you for the pick-up," Piedre winked saucily at me while dangling the villa keys in his hand. I took them from him with two fingers.

"Which way do I go?" I asked, now looking around the classic interior of the lobby. The interior walls were pearl white and grey with warm red and dusty orange rugs to line it. The lobby lounge held ancient looking lamps on end tables nearby, adding warmth to the area. Classic paintings with gold embellished frames hung in the background on one side. I walked a little further and on the other side black and white photos from the past hung. Looked like old shipping ports when I examined closer. The other side of the lobby opened out to the restaurant. I peeped in and a few people were sitting in, eating lunch. My feet were twitching to get out of the lobby. I wanted no part of running into Elliot right now. I could barely breathe. I was steeped in shock.

Piedre pointed to the elevator. "Right upstairs, Madam, then turn to the left. You will see it halfway down the corridor. 13C. I huffed silently, jittering to the elevator. Great, even my villa number was unlucky. My muscles ached as tiredness seeped in. All I wanted now was a nap, and to dream the sight of Elliot away.

I walked to the outside, the dusty gravel swirling around my feet. My villa was a short uphill walk from the reception area. I huffed a little, not enjoying the burn in my legs. I noticed the little wooden sign with 13C on it, leading me inside its walls. I opened the double timber doors, stepping into a mini paradise of tropical flowers and plants with a lit-up walkway. A water feature added to the serenity of it all. I slid the plastic card in my villa front door, releasing out a sigh of relief as I entered. I threw my duffel bag down in tiredness on the carpeted floor. The room was stunning, an all-white backdrop with what looked to be a magnificent freshly made queen bed with a stick of lavender on the pillow. What a nice touch. I strolled over to the balcony and drew back the heavy cream curtains, afraid of the view and the fact it might contain Elliot. But what I saw made me stop and marvel, forgetting all my looming problems. The wide-open expanse of the smooth Tagus River and apricot-tiled rooftops with mostly white and colored buildings of Lisbon. The river was largely clear except for a couple of large cargo ships with tugboats passing through. I drew my gaze closer to the mark and looked down over the pool. There was nobody there.

My attention back to my duffel bag where my clothes were neatly rolled; it gave me more space. I picked out my clothes for the day, heading to the shower to rinse off. Letting the warm water soothe the tension from my weary shoulders, I thought about the madness of it all. The fact that Elliot was so close. The fact that of *all* the hotels and villas that could exist in this place, I'd managed to pick the same one as him. I dried off, dressing quickly as I let my thoughts twist and turn in my head. My stomach growled at me, demanding food. I knew it was time for a Portuguese breakfast. My face switched to a wince as I wasn't keen on going downstairs to ask Piedre for a breakfast spot. I feared getting stuck with him, I needed time to process the notion that the devil was in my backyard.

As I reached for my phone, I heard it beep. I smiled as I thought it might be my parents, my friends or even my long lost sister who was as busy as me. But when I looked at the screen, I put my hand on my now queasy stomach.

Time to play. You thought you got away. That I didn't see you catch the plane. Well guess who's back? A text message from an unknown number and a whole lot of foreign digits. Looked to be a Portuguese number. The first flash of the culprit blazed through my brain. Elliot. *Had to be.* I mean I just saw him at the pool. I felt a cauldron of anger rising from all the sleepless nights and the angst caused due to him. I angrily punched in a text back.

I don't care. I will be the one to take you down. Let's play. An immediate text followed.

Stupid move, little one. Stupid move. Making me angry. Had to be Elliot. I fumbled around with the phone, setting it down. I punched in Hawk's number.

"Hey. I need your help," my breath rapid.

Hawk was calm and silent as he listened. "Okay, go ahead."

"Can you to trace a number for me now. I think Elliot knows I'm here."

"Alright, first step I want you to meet a colleague of mine. I will give you a time and place. You need a weapon."

"Dammit, Hawk! Nothing illegal. I don't want to be caught strapped here. What the hell are you talking about?"

"Facts: Elliot sent an assassin to off Evana, and you were almost killed as well. Now he's potentially sending you text messages, you're in the same villa as the killer. *Think.*"

"Elliot's not going to kill me. He wouldn't do that," my heart tingled as I declared it. Elliot wanted to sleep with me and play with my mind, not kill me. A better way for him to stay above the law and far more brutal.

Hawk sighed. "What? Because you kissed in the café? That's what he does with women. You're playing with a loaded gun," he reminded me with boredom laced in his voice.

"I can handle him. That's not what I need from you right now. Just trace the number. I'll send it to you," I said bossily.

"You know I'm right, that's why you're mad. But yeah, send it." I attached the number and sent it to Hawk.

"I was meant to be exploring the city, now this bullshit."

"You can still do that. Hang on. I'm already set up here. Let's see what I get."

"Hmm. Okay, Nokia phone. It's one of those old school ones. Location Almada. Batikanos Restaurant. Slumming for Elliot." I forcefully pulled the curtain back at the window. No sign of anyone coming or going from the villa. If I didn't take action, I knew it would make me feel like I was helpless.

"Okay. That's all I need to know," I said.

"Back to this are we?"

"Back to what?" I fumed.

"This. Where you go off half-cocked. Remember, I'm the assassin. I might know a thing or two about wielding guns against deadly men."

My internal angst was about to surface and run straight through the phone to Hawk.

"Do you have Portuguese police contacts to bail me out when I shoot Elliot?"

"No. We won't need that."

I ignored him and paced; helped me think sometimes. "Alright, I'm moving on from this conversation. I'm heading out to breakfast."

One of Hawk's calm deadly silences permeated the phone. "See you in a day. I got you covered."

"See you when you get in." I always liked to travel light and be unencumbered as I moved. I did have a little over-the-shoulder satchel, so as soon as I got off the phone with Hawk, I slipped it on. I checked everything in the satchel. I had two phones: my personal and a cheap phone I bought when I landed to talk to Hawk. I also had the little spy device Hawk gave me, my camera with the long lens, pen and paper, plus my converted Euros. I pulled open my villa door and looked both ways. Nothing going. I trudged down the hill to the main reception through a back door. It opened out to the main restaurant. A few people looked up from their breakfast as I charged out of the front. I smoothed my hair down and tilted my face so as not to be seen. My bag swung around my body as I moved my legs as quickly as they could go. I rushed out in the air, gulping it in. This was no way for me to live. If Elliot wanted to taunt me, I wanted to go straight to the source, no more fucking around. Tackle him head on.

On my way I stopped a lady with her trolley bag who was feeding pigeons as I made my way down the declining hill of Almada. No time for scenery intake so much.

"Excuse me. Can you tell me how to get to Batikanos?" I asked slightly out of breath. She was an older lady with a scarf wrapped around her head, she was nibbling on something. Her tired eyes looked at me with a hint of surprise.

"It's down there, right by the ferry. Nice place. Cheap. Near the water. You sit. Enjoy." She smiled then; her mouth filled with gaps from missing teeth.

"Thank you," I heaved. Funny enough, but me moving towards the target made me feel calm. Even though I didn't know if he would still be there. I pulled my camera out of my bag, holding it firmly in my hand. My version of a loaded gun. Photographic evidence. I walked for what seemed an eternity, looked to be forty minutes by my watch. Batikanos sat tucked on a corner. I was walking on the flat now, with no hills in sight. The ferry terminal was in plain view as I looked at the ships docked there.

Loads of people were enjoying the Portuguese ambience, with chairs and tables on the outside of their restaurants. Multicolored terraces sat on both sides. I rolled off a few shoots with my camera. The scene was so uplifting, it brought a long-lost smile to my face. I almost forgot I was there to face Elliot. I looked up to the grimy storefront sign of Batikanos. Two golden donkeys were at the entrance of the restaurant, making it hard to miss. I chuckled a little and snapped a few shots.

One passerby with green eyes said to me, "Funny isn't it?" I nodded with him in agreement. Walking in with a dry mouth I glanced around. No sign of Elliot yet. A strange mix of wanting him to be there and not existed simultaneously in me. People were cajoling, laughing and generally having a good time. I couldn't help but feel better about that. I walked to the front counter timidly.

"Hi, I want to try a Portuguese breakfast." A smiling woman in jeans and stripy top greeted me.

"Of course! Sit wherever you want, and we'll bring it out," I had to stop from the wild goose chase a minute and refuel. He was probably long gone anyway.

I opted for a seat outside to enjoy the clean fresh sea air. My phone beeped violently as I glued my eyes to it.

Too late. I walked right past you. You need to work on your skills. I looked up slowly and scanned the perimeter.

A man with his wife and kid looking into the window of a shop.

A kid dancing in the middle of the cobblestoned path.

A young couple talking intimately, sharing a hot cup of coffee.

Closing my eyes partially I attempted to sense where the threat was coming from. I cast my view up to the buildings above, a lady with dark hair was airing out a blanket on her railed balcony. Sooty windows from sandy colored terrace buildings were closed off. I fought back.

But I knew you were here. Bitch. I wanted to stab whoever this was in the eye. I frowned deeply at the phone. This wasn't the way Elliot spoke to me, but it's the only person it could be...

I made the executive decision to enjoy my breakfast, come what may. My brain told me to act nonchalant. If I showed fear, then it would be the madman's game. I let that sink into my psyche as my breakfast came out. A steaming hot milky coffee in a glass with a red sugar packet, a plate with a Portuguese tart, fried egg, and a croissant with ham and cheese.

"Here you go! Galão, ham and cheese and a sweet treat for you," the waiter said proudly.

"Thanks, this looks delicious, thank you," and it really did. A simple breakfast. Nothing too fancy, but authentic – just what I wanted to experience. I soaked in the elements around me, but a part inside lay coiled, ready to spring into action should I need to. My phone pinged in my pocket as I sipped my milky coffee. I grabbed it out of my pocket. *Hawk.*

"Hullo?"

"Perp is around you. I'm tracing the phone. Look up. That big ship over there. He's somewhere there. I'll check in."

"Okay," I said as I continued to sip my drink.

"Why are you so calm right now? Normally this would cause Ms. Clemens to freak out."

"Because if he's here, then he is. I will deal with it. He can't shoot me in front of this crowd, he'll have to do something to draw me away. That's how I figure. We both know I'm not going for that."

I picked up my ham and cheese croissant that dripped with cheese and watched the buttery flakes fall. I savored the salty and cheesy goodness.

"What are you eating? Sounds good," he asked nosily.

"A croissant."

"In Portugal, figures. Listen you're not invincible. Remember what he's capable of, Sara." That warning shot hit me right in my solar plexus.

"I know. Keep me posted," I added lightly.

"Will do. I hope you got a pastry with that."

I laughed. "I did."

"Bye."

"Bye." I was saving my tart for after the saltiness. A bike

whizzed by with the same man I saw earlier as I walked in. Athletic physique. I noted his hair stood out, it was flaming red. A couple of teenagers that were dressed the same were walking and whispering while looking into their phones. I gave a wistful smile as the wind picked up, blowing my ebony hair across my face. All the while I sat in full target, while the devil watched in the shadows ready to take me out. I have to say I loved it. *I wanted it.* That piece of me that became a P.I. in the first place was rearing to the surface. The thrill of the chase. The heart in the chest moments. The capture. And now in a foreign country when I was far from looking for trouble.

My phone beeped at me. I peered at it. *You missed me again. You really are slipping Ms. Clemens.*

This fucker was pissing me off. I was trying to enjoy my lunch.

If you're going to do something. Go ahead I dare you. Enough, I was calling his bluff. If Elliot was going to play these games then come to the table. Pleased with myself I smiled and crunched down into another piece of my croissant.

Picking up my phone I sent a couple of the selfie shots with the Golden bulls to Hawk. I went back to eating, ten minutes later all I had was my Portuguese tart, the sweet part. Except I didn't get it to my mouth… it was one disturbance after another. My eyes were too busy trying to re-adjust to the sight I just witnessed. From around the corner came two men. One of them was Elliot. *So, it was him, texting,* I concluded. Snatching the tart I threw it in my bag in haste. I got up from the outdoor table as fast as my body could maneuver from the chair. Luckily, I was tucked in the corner table. He had sunglasses on so I couldn't be sure he saw me. I watched as his sexy swagger went by. My body filled with hot naked desire, making my cheeks flush. He was talking in a low voice with what looked to be a local in a Fedora hat. The man slapped him on the back in a friendly way. This man had allies in countries everywhere. I guess that's the life of a billionaire. I was right inside the door window of the restaurant waiting with bated breath. They passed on around the corner. *Shit. Shit. Shit.*

"Are you alright, lady?" A man sitting near the window had obviously been watching me the whole time.

"Yes, I'm fine. All good." Swallowing hard I moved from the space out into the open.

My screen showed a message. *Wrong One.*

A mass of confusion hit my dome. Wrong one? What the hell did that mean? My gut told me it wasn't anything good. I needed answers, so I did what the naughty imp inside me craved.

Follow him, you're going to end up back at the same place anyway...

9

HAWK

"You make me smile. Everything good? I don't need to come and kick anyone's ass?" I asked Evana playfully. I was joking around, *but I wasn't.*

"No, my hunky assassin. You do not. I'm good, but I don't know how long for. I mean, you saw Elliot in Europe. That's what you said, right? He has contacts worldwide. I know for certain. Remember the Columbians? They stayed with us. There were some secret meetings in his chambers that he never let me go into," the tremor in her voice came through the phone.

"I know. I'm aware – that's why I asked. I should have this mark wrapped up today. But it won't end here," I cautioned.

"Ugh."

"We talked about this. This is why I didn't want you involved in the first place, but you wanted to know who I really am, so this is it. It's not a life for the faint hearted. So, if you want to rip my heart out of my chest, let me know now." Pouring it on a little thick, but she needed to know. Out of the norm for me, but she had my heart.

"Hawk, you know I don't want that. That doesn't make it easier, though. The thought of something happening to you... *The danger*. My father... I'm still grieving. I just keep meeting dangerous men." The strain in Evana's voice was evident.

"Well hey, at least this dangerous man will actually protect you from other dangerous men. I know you have a lot to handle. I will be here for you as much as I can. I'm sorry about your father, honey, but that's exactly what I'm working on... It won't happen again. I'm going to put this man out of action."

She let loose a throaty little giggle that I loved. "You get more than a few stars. I want to do some bad things to you when I see you," she replied earthily.

"Promise?" I begged.

"That's an official promise. Problem is: when can I do them? Now I can't come to Portugal because that fucker is there and you got this stuffy bodyguard dude watching me."

"Hey, don't complain about that. I need to make sure you're safe. Let it play out. Technically, the closer you are to me the better I can protect you and make love to you at the same time," I gloated.

"I like a man that can multitask. Let me know what you want to do. I finish my shoot in five days," she said softly.

"I gotta go. I got work to do. Love you, baby. Knock 'em dead. We'll work it out."

"Love you too, Hawk."

"We will work it out," I replied tenderly. I don't know how the hell we worked, but we just did.

My main mission was to sew this mark up. I locked and loaded my semi-automatic, ready for action. I shrugged on my bullet proof vest and secured my gun holster. I slid my tomahawk on the other side. As I laced up my black boots, I reminisced on all the gun shoot outs I'd been in. I'd had some tough calls. Some grazes and nips but never more than that, and I'd been in the assassin game for longer than I cared to remember. It's all I knew. I knew Prince Saeed's location, but he was well and truly covered; it would take an army to get in there.

My watch transmitted the particles that immersed into the Prince's skin providing an infrared read out on my computer. That computer was linked through technology in a watch I wore. It linked the location of the person in question. Some clever advanced spy shit. I'd have to wait 'til he left the location to get at him, but I had enough to go on. Covering myself in a black t-shirt and blue jeans with a non-descript hat, I would say I blended in rather nicely. I took a hard look at myself in the mirror one last time before I left. I raked my fingers through my dark hair as I made my way down the fire escape. I wanted to be a shadow in the night that others couldn't see. Creeping down the cold cement stairs, I knew what I had to do. I could feel the cool strength of my well-tuned body, like a steel blade that I'd trained through years of international engagements, take hold as I went to my car. I drove my vehicle as close as I could to the mosque with one objective only on my mind: one clean kill shot. In my trunk was my sniper rifle, so effectively suppressed, that it was one of the quietest rifles on the planet. I re-checked my watch, concentrating. Prince Saeed was heading back near the mosque. I anticipated his arrival in thirty minutes; this assassin would be a step ahead of him.

My heartrate again, sublimely quiet. All of my senses were on high alert as I cleansed my mind, breathing deep into the bottom of my lungs. I called upon my ancestors in my mind's eye, asking the hawk to come. A vision flashed as the hawk flew in making its presence known. It flapped its coppery wings above the city of Istanbul circling the Rustem Pasha mosque. This I knew is where I needed to be. The hawk gifted me a clear path. I called an Uber arriving at the Spice Bazaar an hour ahead of schedule, wanting to set up. Inside my drag bag was the sniper rifle with all its contents.

Gliding through the Spice Bazaar, I picked up a trinket here or there to dampen suspicion. Nobody knew about the supersonic that could take out civilians like sitting ducks as I ducked and weaved through the crowd. Next up, access to the mosque roof. No part of me could think complacently, as Prince Saeed could be armed. Once I shot him, I had to move. The other two would suspect and either come looking or run. Better if I picked him off before the lead up to the mosque. Time to move like a wolf in the stolen deep of the night. My aim was airtight. I never missed, and if I did it was on purpose. Thoughts of Evana drifted in, longing to touch her silken skin. The faster I got this over with the faster I could get to my girl.

The scene was like a rerun from the last time at the market. Tourists and locals were floating in and out of stalls. Retailers were hawking their wares. A smile danced over my lips at the cultural diversity as I avoided eye contact with civilians, moving through casually. My eyes scanned over the crowd as I searched for the Prince. Checking my watch, the radar beeped letting me know he was close by. Just over 200 yards away. The heat was amplified by the number of people in the bazaar. I always made a loose plan, not holding it too close to my heart as plans for assassins never really worked out. They shifted and changed depending on the players, and right now I had a lot of them. The bazaar parted like the Red Sea as Prince Saeed himself strode through, his self-impor-tance on full blast. People stood back a little, even though they didn't have any clue who he was. A hundred yards and closing. My eyes fixated on the Prince; again he was wrapped in white with a gold belt around him. His other Arabian friend strode in time with him. King Abodowie with his red and gold cap and matching cloth strode through the bazaar as people snapped pictures. The King obliged by puffing out his chest and waving with a single palm – he, too, keeping stride with his killers.

They were about to be one man down with nobody to make a deal with. I slid like a fox behind a crowd of people. Nobody cared, they were busy talking amongst themselves and deciding on things to buy. The targets moved to the contrasting stillness of the mosque. I headed them off by entering the stairwell on the side, moving like a stealthy ninja to the rooftop. I knew the layout inside out as I studied the map. The ottoman who designed the mosque layout was a master builder, the building being constructed in 1563. Would be a shame if I missed and put a bullet hole in the pretty place. In the top of the steeple's alcove, I would sit like a game cat waiting for its prey. I heard them talking in Arabic, conversing as if not a care in the world. Miguel had joined them, just like last time. Now the English commenced. I was above them now inside the roof lining, setting up to shoot between the cracks. I had enough room for the euthanasia bullet to skim through.

"Ah Miguel, so glad you could make it. We wanted to talk to you about the American ports before you leave back to your home country," Prince Saeed greeted with enthusiasm.

Miguel's rich Portuguese accent flavored his tone. "Yes, of course. I have confirmed with the American that we can deliver by the end of the month. You can give your Russian counterparts the green light."

King Abodowie let out a rumbling belly laugh. "This is one hell of a deal, it will allow me to take over those pesky militant armies that have been plaguing us for the last three months in the Congo." I unpacked silently, locking my sniper gun in position. I didn't want to get too comfortable. This was a hit him and run scenario.

An eerie laugh came from Prince Saeed. "See, as we envisage greater things for our countries, we can achieve them. I will make sure you have no problems moving through the Middle East or these quarters. No need to worry from this end."

You have plenty to worry about. It's your time to die now and eat these bullets.

From my vantage point, King Abodowie had his back to me. Prince Saeed was closest to me, also with his back to my gun. Miguel in his aloofness was wandering around the small space, looking around. The other Arab man I didn't have a name for, looked to be Prince Saeed's tag-along. He didn't have the physique of a bodyguard at all and was small in stature. He stood with his hands behind his back. I made the tiniest of shifts to angle my gun. I didn't ask too many questions of Homeland Security. I was asked to take out one man only at this point. The others I could shoot if they posed a problem.

"Only shoot the others if you need to, Hawk. We want to send a message. We want them scared. We want them to feel the heat."

"Won't that just make them more careful? Don't you want them complacent?"

"They won't tighten up. They will just find new avenues. They will need to regroup and that will give us time to work on taking down their operation."

"If you say so."

Squinting, I looked through the target hole with my hand on the trigger, all I needed to do was squeeze. The shot, crystal clear. I had the whole target of Prince Saeed's head.

The others were away from him now. Slight gaps on either side. I opened my backpack ready for a quick pack down. I knelt on one knee, refocusing on the target. Closing my eyes, I composed my breath. The Grim Reaper was about to deliver. The bullet flew at breakneck speed through the crack. I knew it hit. A clean shot right through the middle of the skull. I clicked the sniper gun in position packing with lightning precision. The cry of a man down and a resounding thud rang out. One I'd heard so many times.

A quick glance saw the others look up to the roof. Prince Saeed had fallen forward, three large spots of vibrant red blood spread through his finely woven clothing. By that time I'd packed down. I unlocked the semi, ready for confrontation just in case. They had to figure out how to get to the roof. I'd locked the door and there was only one entrance to me. I heard the furious jangling of the door.

"Hey motherfucker!! He's on the roof. Quick!" Miguel spat, angrily. I was on the move. The faster I got to the bazaar the better, into the crowd to mingle. My heart thumped loudly. I moved through the winding staircase with lightning quick feet.

King Abodowie's booming voice rang through. "How did this happen! Who did this?"

All voices were intermingled now as they struggled to comprehend that Prince Saeed had been shot.

While I still heard them playing with the door, I eased my speed as I reached the bottom, placing my semi in my holster, slinking through the bazaar without being followed. Job done. Just like that. Relatively clean. I hailed for an Uber straight back to my hotel for the next part of the fight. *Elliot.*

10

ELLIOT

☖

That smooth caramel skin, those full ripe lips. I would know them whatever country I travelled to. Reliable sources told me she was in the country ahead of time. I caught a glimpse of her thick ebony hair as soon as she arrived at the villa. Just a matter of time before we crossed paths. I was biding my time, plotting her erotic take-down. My deviant heart skipped a beat as my cock elevated at the sight of her near the restaurant. My sunglasses were dark as night so she never would've known if I saw her or not. But she was one I couldn't miss. A radar deep in my soul went off when Ms. Clemens was nearby. I was with Fabio; he decided to stay on in the city for a few days and we were enjoying a lazy Portuguese brunch. She'd tucked herself in a café corner discreetly, waiting for me to pass. I knew she wouldn't be able to help herself. She would follow me. She had this intense, intriguing curiosity that couldn't keep her away from me. I knew she thrived on the game – that she wanted me as much as I wanted her. I would play her right into my muscular arms and into my villa bed. Months of waiting, cursing myself for not bedding her in New York. I wanted to devour every single inch of her svelte body, to taste her other set of lips. To hear her moan my name in tortuous pleasure. Once I claimed the P.I. she would be tied to me: mind, body and soul.

A door at the back of my heart was being knocked on, but I refused to open it. I had too much darkness clouding the front of it, but for some reason a crack of light appeared with her. As we turned the corner we waited for Fabio's driver to arrive. Inside, my core burned with a molten lava of desire. I could sense her. I kept my sunglasses on, but my onyx eyes searched frantically for her behind the glasses. They penetrated the Almada crowd. Ms. Clemens was just the right height for me and those long, toned legs deserved the pleasure of being wrapped around me. The thunder in my chest wouldn't let up as I stood beside Fabio.

"Are you okay, Elliot?" Fabio dragged me away from my thoughts. The change in my energy must have been clear.

"Yeah. I'm good. I have some things to take care of, is all," I noted quickly.

"Está bem," Fabio replied. "My girl will be here soon. You come visit me in Columbia. See the operation first hand," Fabio gestured enthusiastically.

"Your girl, huh? Are you a taken man now, Fabio?"

The Columbian drug lord pushed his multiple rings further down on his fat fingers with a pensive look.

"There comes a time in every man's life when he has to wind down his activities a little." He made a wavy hand gesture back and forth as if balancing the scales. "We have a baby girl now, and you know I have a few to take care of…" He backhanded me on the chest with a leery grin. "You know how it is, right? Never one, but I got a little less these days. Not as many headaches."

"Oh, trust me: one can cause you a headache," I responded in wry amusement. I watched as the crowd of tourists and locals intermingled along our path. A shiny black Mercedes pulled up across the road with the window rolled down.

"That's true... We'll be in touch. Get yourself a nice Portuguese lady while you're here." He winked his scheming eye at me as I observed his leathery crow's feet bunch together when he smiled.

"That's already taken care of, except she's not Portuguese," I kept my gaze straight ahead. I didn't know where Ms. Clemens was, but she had my blood pumping and I loved it.

Fabio's husky laugh in reply made me think about the present I was about to unravel. One I'd been waiting for. "Nice. Bye, my friend."

"Bye, Fabio – be in touch soon," I said. A young lady with long dark hair and tanned skin waved at me out the window. I waved back at her. I watched as the smoke billowed from the exhaust and Fabio drove off with one of his harem.

My focus returned. I knew her room number. Piedre had given it to me. I knew she was watching. Now *this* was a game I lived for.

Sara, you're going to be mine. I know you're watching, and now is the time. We are long overdue, baby.

My loins ached for her, but not like for other women. This was entirely different. A new feeling, one of protection, lust, and an emotion I didn't want to admit to myself out loud. I never wanted her to be involved with Evana that closely. It's why I wanted her to come work for me. She would have been a useful ally. I didn't want the Viper to go near her. One of Clope's lunatic contacts. I stayed out of it when Clope organized a hit. One, so I wasn't implicated; and two, because I didn't care to know. That's what I paid him for. To clean up the mess and dispose of it.

I frowned momentarily as the wind from the wharf blew an icy gust over my face. Clope had fucked up the Michael

Sawyer issue, he'd messed up with the Viper. Evana was still out there, with some of my fraudulent secrets. She didn't know all of them, but the ones she did know were deadly. If it got out about Cluster Ferman, it would ruin my whole port operation. The other things, like the secret family meetings she had no clue about, my father made sure.

"This is men's business. No women allowed. We have a legacy to protect. Besides, your wife isn't exactly legacy material. She's hard dick material. You need to get rid of her." My father could be cutthroat at times. But if you were his blood, he would defend you to death. A calm came over my body because I knew I was in control.

Ricardo showed up, interrupting my plotting. I opened the sleek town door.

"Ricardo, good to see you. Trust your day has been going well."

"Pretty good boss. I got a little news for you," he said as I slid in back. "You were right to feel a little edgy about Miguel. Apparently, he has some shadier connections in terms of arms dealings. I overheard a conversation from a pick up the other night." Ricardo, with his dark slicked back hair, gave me a look in the mirror.

I rubbed my hands together at the news. "I see. That's altogether interesting. Might be time to strike a deal," I said, lifting my glass to my head.

"Careful with him. He has some global connections that will blow you away. That's not from anyone, that's from me personally. He has relatives that work with the consulate."

My jaw tightened as I thought about the Portuguese weasel trying to double cross me.

"Don't worry about that. My familia will take care of it. We run deeper than he knows."

Ricardo looked in the mirror, saluting. "Thought so. I knew you would have an answer for the situation," he smirked.

"My man. Good job. Keep on it," I responded curtly. My plants were everywhere, crawling out of every gloomy nook and cranny around the globe. Not a single enemy was safe around me. The town car rolled smoothly into the villa entrance, coming to a slow halt. My entrance was separated from the other visitors and half a mile away from the main hotel. The Alamada wind had picked up, and I could see the reception palms moving freely with the breeze.

"Of course. Of course. No problem. Are you planning on heading out this evening or staying in?" Ricardo enquired.

"No, I'll be staying in," I replied with a slick smile. Only I knew the magic of why. I opened my door, stretching out tall as I got out of the vehicle. I made my way inside my spacious villa as the wind whistled and soft rain droplets peppered the cinnamon-colored dirt. My breathing heightened as I knew I was one step closer to taking down my prey. This prey I didn't want to kill. I wanted to subdue and immobilize. I glided up the winding staircase with precise strides, wrestling with a powerful appetite that needed to be whet by Ms. Clemens. I'd turned down hot ass because of her. She wouldn't regret the Robert Elliot experience, I smirked. I wanted to leave my carnal imprint on her soul, so she would never forget no matter what happened between us. As I opened the balcony door to the outside I looked across through the thin sheets of rain to the main building. Time to unfold my plans. I picked up the old school villa phone, calling down to reception. "Yes, hello can you please send a bottle of Dom Perignon to Villa number 13? Along with strawberries and whipped cream."

Piedre's croaky outbreak of laughter rang through the phone. "Of course, sir, with pleasure. She is a beauty, isn't she?"

"That she is, tell her it's from an old friend," my tone held warning. I knew how he exploited Isabella. I would crush his skull with my bare hands if he even thought for a minute of touching Sara.

Piedre's laughter was in full bloom now. "As you wish Mr. Elliot. Anything else you would like to send?"

"No, I can do the rest." *Because I could.* I would give her some time. Let her think that's all the night would gift her. She would know it was from me. I moved to the huge open shower, stripping off my clothes, letting the hot water soak my well-built frame. I imagined Ms. Clemens standing under the shower with me, me, fondling her supple caramel breasts as she arched her back. The mere thought of her made my blood rush hot with desire. She was mine for the taking. I dried off, shaved, changed into a crisp white linen shirt with slate grey slacks. I wanted to look the part for her. This wasn't the time to be casual. This was to be an experience of a lifetime that Ms. Clemens would never forget. They didn't call me the panty dropper for no reason. I tamed my dark hair with a teardrop of gel. I observed as my unruly hair laid obediently into place. The last ritual involved a dab of cologne. I knew she adored my scent. I cocked a half smile at myself in the oval mirror, silently moving from my room to go get my woman.

My heart pounded in my chest as I sneaked through to the oak doors of her enclosed villa. As I walked through the white arched entryway, I took note of the surrounding flowers. A nice touch of romanticism. I rapped my knuckles on her solid wooden door three times.

I knew for a fact there were no peepholes on the doors. I waited patiently for her to answer.

"Who is it?" she asked in an accusatory tone.

"The best thing you've ever known in your whole life," I countered in my rich velvety voice. She stopped for a beat as I heard her click the magazine of her gun in place. "Loaded, I see. I expected nothing less. I'm not going to hurt you, baby. You got the champagne on ice I sent you?" I slid down the door and sat, waiting. Might take a while, but I would wear her down.

"Real slick, Elliot. So, you skipped the country, huh?" she snarked. I licked my lips, confident I had her right where I wanted her. She was mad, even better. More passion, better lovemaking, she was dancing right into my trap.

"Did you get my note?" I asked in a low tone. I heard her knocking things around and rustling something. Made me frown as I strained to listen. I was pretty comfortable as I sat on the welcome mat right out front. I let my arm drape over my raised knee.

"I got it. You're right we have unfinished business. Me making an arrest and getting you back on American shores," she spat.

I chuckled a little, touching my hand to the grainy wood door. "You don't have anything on me, so how can you bring me back to the country? I haven't been charged with a goddamn thing," I countered. *This was fun.* I wondered how uptight she was, how bad she wanted me.

"Are you sitting outside my door, Robert?" Her barbed question tickled me.

"Yes, Ma'am – I am. I'll wait all night if I have to. I just wanna talk. I don't have any weapons. You're the one with the gun," I added lightly tapping my head against the door.

"Shhh, keep your voice down. You know why the fuck I have it?" she hissed.

"You tell me? Because if I remember correctly, that's not how you and I are doing things." I rolled my tongue around in my mouth as the fire of explosive passion I harbored for this mysterious woman threatened to unhinge me. I felt my cock getting hard from her voice. She was a red flag for a treacherous soul like me and I loved it. I heard her short breaths. I listened intently for it.

The oxygen she craved to give her a reprieve from the resistance she was denying.

The desperation was in her tone.

We possessed a telepathic bond, the good side and the bad side locked in magnetic battle.

"I have it because of you. You sent that motherfucking *thing* after me. You bastard!" She shot out. I dropped my head a little rolling my neck around. Second round.

"*Correction*, you decided to chase my whore of a wife and found yourself in a bad situation. Sorry, honey – can't blame that one on me. I told you to come work for me," I warned with a terse tone.

"*What?* I was just going to *let* you kidnap your wife?"

"Ha!. Nice try. I don't know what you're talking about. But, hey let's talk about us. You enjoy your breakfast this morning? Looked good. I wish I could have joined you."

I heard the sharp intake of her breath and grinned. "You are an asshole, Elliot."

"Yeah, but you wanna let the asshole in. I'm not a threat to you like I said. I just want to spend some time with you. I won't tell if you don't. Just hear me out. Stop chasing me like a wild animal. You don't need to. I'm right here, sexy. *Isn't this what you wanted?* I sure as hell have..." I rocked her to sleep with my pleading sensual tone. The pressure between us was rising. My instincts told me to get up off the floor. I rose up slowly and her villa door creaked opened. Face to face with Ms. Clemens, her chocolate eyes staring right into mine. Her face appeared to be cold, but I knew better. In a swift and deadly move, I grabbed her pretty face with both hands, crushing my mouth against hers. I kicked the door closed behind me. I let up for only a second as she moved back into the apartment and I moved in time with her. Her small desperate pants let me know everything.

"Damn, I want you. Now let me make you come all night long," I growled. I let my hot breath and horny voice ring in her ear.

An involuntary moan escaped her as I continued the

assault on her plump lips. I sucked on her bottom lip, weaving my long tongue with hers. The heat from our mouths flamed the animalistic urges contained in both of us. Both her fists were balled on my toned chest. I still had a gentle grip on the curves of her face. Slowly, she beat her fist on my chest like a drum.

"Fuck you, Elliot," she said passionately. She was caving in. I resumed the slow breakdown of her weakened defenses as she kissed me back with fervor.

There it was. All was not lost.

"Now that's more like it. Talk to me, baby." I breathed in delicious anguish. My cock was rammed hard into the side of her thigh as I moved my hands down the length of her, skimming her breasts. "Mmmm," she responded in pleasure. Her arms were around my neck now, her chocolate eyes turned to liquid, soft and inviting. "Hi, there. I missed you." I reduced the pace, giving her time to absorb where I wanted to take her.

"How long have you been planning this?" Her face upon first look appeared to be an open book, but I knew different. I knew she was a welcome match for me. Adrenaline had my heart racing.

"The whole time. I knew you were coming. I've been waiting for you. You look good." She smiled giving me a dopey grin. I surprised her by lifting her up, and she instinctively wrapped her legs around me. Strong, powerful and light all in one. Her scent, intoxicating.

"How did you know? You really should put me down. This is all kinds of wrong. You're not even divorced yet, and I'm friends with your missing wife. Let alone all the other reasons why. Including your criminal activities."

My dark eyes burned into hers, "And not a single one of those reasons stopped you from opening the door to me," I replied, burrowing my head into her neck. I searched out her villa for the champagne.

"Shall we have a drink together? I see you haven't opened it," I said as I took off my shoes and padded to the tray pouring the bubbly wheat-colored liquid in two glasses. I handed one to her as I watched her breasts moving up and down from ragged breath. She took it with shaky fingers and sipped. Part of the liquid dribbled on the side of her caramel-hued chin. I made good use of it, crossing to her. "Let me help with that."

I didn't give her time to think. I lapped it up with my silvery tongue and continued to kiss her.

"I don't know what the fuck you're doing here, Elliot." She was still vying to be mad, but she was failing miserably.

"Yes, the fuck you do," I reasoned with darkened eyes. A devilish smile curled on her lips as we both sipped more champagne. She nodded in understanding. I watched her perfect full lips drink as she put it to the side, with her glass half full. I followed suit.

Her feminine softness wafted in and I saw visible signs of her walls drop. More of the dark fog in front of my heart cleared. She wasn't the only one in danger. So was I, and this isn't how I imagined it to be. The tenderness I felt for her stopped me from ravaging her. I wanted to caress her soul. To sprinkle kisses all over her smooth, enticing skin.

"A mistake," she reiterated without conviction. I reached for her, cupping her bottom as she stood facing me with my firm hard on intact. I could wait. Nothing would make my cock deflate anyway. Not with the ferocity of passion I felt inside of me for Sara. All I could read in her face was the same voracious energy I had. My gaze fastened on her lips as I took them again, slower this time, with care. I watched her eyelids flutter as she gave herself to me. We drew back from one another, silent urgent breaths causing both of our chests to ascend and fall.

"No mistake, Sara. Not a fucking chance of a mistake, and you know it. You can't turn back now. We're in it. Tell me something real... *Do you want me or not?* If you can lie well enough to yourself, then I'll leave," I lied. I was going nowhere, but I was pretending to give her the option.

"Why are you doing this? Why couldn't you just leave me alone and fuck the next woman, like I'm sure you've already done since you've been here." Every word that dripped from Sara's plump lips sounded like the pure seduction of a kitty cat.

My hooded eyes tunneled into hers. "You're not just that to me. *This* is something else. I know you're dangerous, maybe you're recording everything. I don't know. But I know I'm willing to put it on the line to have you. I know it's impossible. I know you think I mean you harm. But I don't. I'll defend you. I'll make sure nothing happens to you. Come away with me. Just live this life with me." The offer of a lifetime for many, but not for this private investigator. I knew she wouldn't take it. She had too much of a justice streak and pride in her.

"Do you know what you're offering? What do you think I'm going to do, Robert? Sit around and be your little play toy? There's not a snowball's chance in hell." Her cute nose wrinkled and words spoke of fire, but I'd soon extinguish it. I gave her a flirty smile.

"I never said anything like that. I admire your independent spirit, I just want you in my bed every night. To wake up with you," No word of a lie came from my lips in that moment. She paused, staring at me.

"This one time and that's it. A memory. Let's get this out of our systems," she reasoned softly.

My cock got even harder as I zoned back in on her lips, taking them. I swung her around and sat her on my lap. I'd walked her to the bedroom without her even realizing. The bed rebounded under us. She straddled me, starting a slow grind, I released a guttural moan of wretched desire that I'd held inside for the last six months. "Mmmm, you little minx. *No no no.* Come here."

I flipped her from the intimate clench we were in and turned her onto the bed gently. "This has to go." I slid both my large hands up her body, lifting her top over her head. She looked like an angel lying there, surrendering to me. Underneath, the swell of her breasts were covered with a red silken bra, her nipples hardened. I lightly grazed one with my finger over the material, closing my eyes, savoring her. Sara moaned in delight, her mouth open. I moved to the other side, running my palm over the erect tip, kneading and caressing. I leaned my head forward, replacing hands with my mouth blowing hot air through her bra. "*Love this.* How did you know I like silk?" I asked. I reached behind deftly taking off her bra, throwing it to the side. I gazed upon the goddess as I took each wonderful mound in my mouth. She sucked in air as I kneaded each, teasing her with my tongue, rolling it over her sensitized buds over and over. One by one.

"I don't know if I can take this," she pleaded as she writhed underneath me. I pulled up for a moment, unbuttoning my shirt. Her eyes widened as she touched her fingertips to my bare, tightly muscled chest. They felt like pads of pure electricity coursing through my dark veins.

"Robert," she breathed seductively.

"Take it easy, breathe for me. Let me take you on a ride, baby. If this is all we have let's make it last," I replied with a raspy whisper. She turned her head to reveal the curve of her neck, needy in glorious torture.

The sheets moved with her as I grinned in the shadows as night fell on us. The rain was starting to play its music on the terrace rooftop, everything feeling just right. "Let's see what else I can investigate," I probed.

She giggled delicately as I smiled through the darkness with her. Sensual and mesmerizing, I wanted to remember every juncture with her. I would give her as much as I could.

After all I was a man on the run as much as I pretended to deny it. I focused on the creme brûlée in front of me. I moved her jeans to the floor, unzipping them first and yanking them from her thighs. A red silk g string was my treat. I wasted no time. I ran my hand shakily from the bottom of her swan-like throat; she responded by arching her back for me. I flicked my tongue out as I concentrated, keeping my fingers running over her in a vertical line straight to the hot essence of her slick center. I circled my hand over the silk; *damn that felt good.* She cried out hungrily. I pushed the g-string to the side to reveal her slick entrance, dripping wet for me. I gently probed with two fingers and ran my fingers back around to her ultimate pleasure spot.

"Stop, you're torturing me," she breathed, her face twisted in exquisite agony.

"No, baby. I'm just getting warmed up. We haven't started yet, believe me." My hoarse throaty voice was overwhelmed with a phenomenal craving that scared the shit out of me. Every fiber in my being had to hang on tight not to ravish her. I breathed slowly with steady control. I started back at the top, fluttering fiery kisses along her torso, hot scorching kisses. She giggled in spots and clutched the sheets with tempestuous yearning in others. My hair fell over her smooth body, grazing her stomach. I took her g-string off and she spread her legs for me. I kissed one side of her inner thigh, nibbling, sucking, internally reveling in the fact I was making love to the most dangerous enemy to me on the planet. I wouldn't let up with the slow torture.

She kept bucking, trying to make me go to the center of her, which was dying for my touch. I grabbed her leg to stop her from wriggling, then rewarded with a caress. Her panting increased and so did mine. I moved to the other delicious inner thigh. I couldn't leave it longing. The sheets were wet from both of our primal energies, desperately wanting to merge. Finally, I dipped my head into her blazing feminine paradise, my tongue diving in headfirst, working the middle of her crevices circling in and out. Sara's throaty cries unleashed the torrid craving she buried and tried to hide from me. But she couldn't run anymore. Now I knew in the shadowy light of her villa. The feeling was *entirely* mutual. Her curvaceous body propelled into overdrive as I increased pace, then dropped her, letting up, taking her to the brink and back again. I took her out of her misery as I explored the upper lids of her folds and pressed on her aching, swollen nub. She released a howl of ecstasy as I watched the wave of orgasmic bliss roll over her.

"Ohhh my god!" she sang out joyfully. Both of us were slicked in sweat, my chest moving in and out. I dropped my pants as my erection sprang forward. The second time I watched her eyes widen as I allowed the joyride of pleasure to subside. My cock glistened, ready to enter the promised land. I pulled a condom out of my pocket and slid it on discreetly. I patted the sides of my shoulders.

"Put your legs up here, baby," I coaxed gently.

I kissed her manicured feet on the way up as she slid her ass to me and lifted her long legs to my shoulders. I gritted my teeth to hold onto my slipping control. I slowly dipped my length into her hot, fisted glove. Her internal walls stretched beautifully around me. The dark primal earthiness in me wanted to take over, to make her suffer in the most unbearable erotic way. I resisted and moved my hips in wave-like motions rocking her into submission. I watched as her toffee-colored breasts moved in time with me as I grabbed one, squeezing lightly. "I knew you wanted me," I breathed. "*I knew it.*" I felt victorious, until she tightened her inner walls around me and pushed down on my cock with force. My mouth came open as she squeezed.

"Sara, fuck, wait, baby." She grinned salaciously as I worked her some more, sweat running like a waterfall down my chest. My pace became more frenzied as the earthy wildness in her came to the forefront.

"Take me to the edge, Robert. Take me," she groaned. That was my cue, this wasn't the end – just round one. My cock hardened ready to explode as I grabbed her ass, she matched my rhythm and intensity as I artfully thrust my way to a powerful heart-wrenching orgasmic release.

She released with me as we both let go from the grip we were holding one another in. Sara laid back gasping for air and so did I.

"Round one down. Round two coming up. But let's eat first."

11

SARA

♟

Erotic moments so thickly etched in time that they couldn't be erased. The killer of many occupying my Portuguese villa bed. Now my body was filled with the energy of a ruthless billionaire, and to be brutally honest it never felt so good. The man was a phenomenal lover. I understood his reputation now. Room service, and then round two of lovemaking ensued. Afterwards, I laid on my back, my whole-body throbbing in sated pleasure. The guilt hadn't set in at that point, but I knew it would once he left. My arms were stretched above my head as Elliot leaned on his elbow, with his thickly muscled chest and dark charcoal pupils zooming in on me.

"Did you think it would be cute to send me messages? Was that part of the chase as well?" I asked casually as he stroked my naked skin.

"Hmm. No, I didn't send any messages. I saw you already at the reception desk." He frowned, looking upon me in appreciation.

I looked long and hard at him, studying his movements

for any hint of a lie. His frowning told me he was being serious, but I still probed just in case.

"C'mon, you can at least tell me that much... You didn't
send those messages to me?"

"No. I didn't. I told you. I saw you already. I knew where
you were. I cut straight to the chase. No need for an appetizer
when I have the main course." Robert confirmed as he circled
my belly button causing butterflies to flit around. I sat up
quickly raising the sheets to my breasts.

"You didn't?" Elliot combed a hand through his unkempt
hair as he sat his well-defined frame up to me.

"I promise you. I didn't – I have no problem telling you
that. The last thing I wrote to you was the letter I left under
your bed."

I tilted my head at him. "How the hell did you leave that
note by the way? You were already out of the country."

A slippery smile curved on his magnificent lips. I wanted
to kiss them again, but I held off. "That's for me to know and
you never to find out, sweet thing."

"You're kidding me, right?"

"Nope. Back to this text message situation. What did one
of them say? Read it out to me..." Elliot asked thickly.

"Well one of them said you walked right past me," the
sated feeling had worn off a little and was slowly being
replaced with a looming panic.

"Sara. I can assure you I didn't send it," Elliot with his
iceberg blue eyes solemnly replied.

My mood changed like a wafting cloud over the moon. "I
know you sent it. You did walk right past me around about the
same time," I pressed as I sat up.

Robert smiled with resignation at me. "Alright, if that's
going to shut you up. Then I'll run with it. It was me that sent
you the message," He licked my neck and I shivered from the
tickle of it.

"*Stop.*" I hit him lightly on the arm. "You know you have

to go now right? You know we can never see one another again."

Nightfall came over Elliot's face. "Why? Come away with me. Be with me, Sara. Before you say no at least think about it. *Really think about it*. This isn't the end for us."

Elliot stole the breath from my mouth as he crashed into my lips like a riptide out to sea, plundering, and plunging just like the waves. The man's magnetism would bring any woman to their knees. I breathed in deep to regain the lost oxygen Elliot took from my lungs, immersing myself in his blue eyes.

"We can't Robert. We are on two different sides of the law. I know which one I live on," I justified.

"Do you, Sara? Because you just crossed over to the dark side with me. Sometimes life isn't black and white. You can play in the grey area. See me again." Robert's husky tone made me want to jump him as he seductively stroked my arm, goosebumps rising in plain view.

"No. I can't. I'm sorry. I just can't," I replied sorrowfully getting lost in the blueness of his eyes. Maybe there was love there... *Just maybe*. I was mixed up inside.

"Can't or won't, Sara?" Robert asked coldly.

"Won't." I stroked his cheek softly enjoying the prickles from his two o'clock shadow.

"Tell me Robert, what happened to Michael?" I narrowed my eyes and moistened my lips. This was a dangerous playground and right now I was riding on the carousel.

"So, you can trap me on a recording?" I opened my mouth to plead my case. He put a finger to my lips and stopped me. "No, Sara. We aren't doing that... Screw semantics. What you and I have is greater than our problems, otherwise you wouldn't have just let me fuck you back to front like that."

I stretched out my legs under the cool white sheets. "Might be a grain of truth to what you're saying, but I still have to ask you."

Robert nodded with his sly megawatt smile. "I'm pretty mild compared to my billionaire counterparts. Trust me. We'll get together again. I look forward to the next chase, Ms. Clemens. Until then, take care. Try not to fall for too many criminals," He winked as I noted the sadness in his eyes.

"You are trouble. You gotta go," I retorted in a teasing tone.

"One that likes to satisfy you to no end," he stated. Robert elevated his godly presence from the bed as I admired the roundness of his firm buttocks and tight hamstrings. I watched as he slipped on his underwear, then his pants and shirt. He grabbed the pen and a piece of paper on the side desk, scribbling on it. He slid his hand through his hair and looked back.

"Well you're pretty good at it. I can't complain," I added peacefully, but a tiny knot was forming in my stomach about him not sending the text message.

"That's what I thought. If you need me, just call. Could be two weeks of pure heaven for you, if you let me cater to you. I can take you on a tour to see the real Portugal, and we could have all kinds of fun. Think about it." Robert's icy pale eyes pounced on mine as I looked down at the sheets. His tenderness was making me unsettled.

"We've already crossed the line. That's it," I said. I looked up at him through my long lashes with the sting of regret.

He stood near the side desk with his crisp white shirt wide open at the neck. I bit my lip; he looked undeniably sexy. "No regrets," I said, trying to clear it up.

"Good," he said simply. As I watched the back of him leave, I felt a gloominess creep up inside of me. What I did was all kinds of twisted. But I didn't care, I had to have the Robert Elliot experience just once. It could be our little naughty secret. I laid back on my bed languishing in the beauty of the man's deft touch. The way he caressed and satisfied every inch of my body in ways I'd only dreamed of. I gritted my teeth momentarily; so many clues I wanted to get from him.

I wanted to ask him about his university hustle.

I wanted to know how he got away with it.

I knew instinctively he ordered the hit on that student reporter.

I just knew it, but I was caught up. The imp had taken over my body and I was damn happy she did.

I lazily made my way to the shower, washing away the remnants of passionate lovemaking, knowing the memory would forever permeate my soul and mind. As I lathered on the coconut villa soap, I thought about what he said about the text message. Was he playing with me?

As I stepped out and towel dried off, I contemplated. The buzz of my phone going off made me jolt a little. I wrapped the towel around my waist hastily and grabbed my phone. A picture message from Hawk. He'd blown up the photo I sent to him in front of the Golden bulls at the wharf. The photo had a red circle around it with a guy who'd ridden his bike past me. Long pointy nose.

Dark soulless eyes looking straight at me.

Small weedy build.

Holy fucking shitballs.

It was the fucking Viper.

My eyes ran to the next line on my phone. *Recognize anyone? Strap up needed. Don't let anyone in your room. I mean it. No one.*

My body went into fight or flight mode. I gathered myself, quickly put some panties on along with my bra. I wriggled into my jeans and threw a tee on. My brain in its sex-filled fog quickly lifted. I pursed my lips together. Now I saw why Hawk was right about getting a gun, and I'd ignored his advice. I was defenseless in this beautiful, classically decorated villa. Powerless to stop the Viper from getting to me. All of the text messages would have only incited him.

I picked up the phone calling Hawk, the international dial code patched through. He answered tersely, "I'm on the way. Next plane out. I want you to lock all the windows and doors. I'm going to send a colleague to you, just in case I can't make it in time."

"Why the fuck is this guy still after me? He got his fucking money, right?" I hissed with frightful anger.

"Well even if he did, he's a twisted fuck. For some assassins, payment or not, they want to finish the job. The guy I'm going to send is called Raul. He has black hair, a big bodybuilder build. He will knock three times. He's going to bring you some firepower. Squeeze the trigger. Don't hesitate. I'm 15 hours away. Call you on the land. Call me as many times as you need. I'll see if I can get a tracker on this cell phone number," he said quickly.

Dizzy from the sickening alarm I said, "Hurry, Hawk."

I walked around the villa, looking at the seals on the windows. Pressing my fingers into the corners, I moved to the modern open bathroom, checking for possible entry points. Not one. I raced to the front door and peeked my head out. I could see the other villas next to me. All of them had a lot of plant cover and high white rendered walls for privacy.

I jumped five feet in the air as my phone violently beeped again. Every time it did it felt like a tripwire went off inside of me.

Have a nice time with your lover? This story just gets better doesn't it?

My hands trembled, sending my nerve endings into a scattered frenzy. I steadied my breath. To me, this meant he was close by. He could see me, or he saw Elliot and was making assumptions. One of the two. Either way, both options were bad. I ran to the villa kitchen and grabbed the steak knife out of it. Come what may at least I wouldn't go down without a fight. ~~15~~ Fifteen fucking hours away. *What the fuck.*

I pressed the call button to Hawk. "He knows I'm here."

"Receive a message?"

I bit my lip, perturbed. "Yeah, how'd you know?"

"I'm tracking him, via the phone. Careful though – could be a diversion. He might have handed the phone to someone else."

"Fuck, Hawk! Why can't I just have a clear-cut answer with you?"

Hawk laughed wildly. "Assassins are rarely straightforward; it's what makes us great at the job. Stay focused, Raul is close by. In fact, you should hear three knocks right now."

I gulped down my fear, panting, and my tongue dry. Three hard knocks at the door made me blink hard, again jumping in the air. A common symptom of bad men chasing me.

I swung the door open and a hard-muscled guy with dark midnight eyes stared back at me. One of his arms was the size of both of mine. He wore all black. I still had my mobile cradled in my hand.

"Umm. Hawk he's here – gotta go."

"'Kay."

Raul's hard line square jaw lifted into a lopsided grin. "Heard you needed some assistance?"

I scanned him quickly. I heard a slight scuffling sound, except I didn't know where it was coming from. I ignored it and focused on the man taking up my whole villa doorway. Raul heard it too and looked up to the villa rooftop. "Move back from the door," he said in a deathly smooth voice. Startled, I inched back.

"Shit. What is it?"

I noticed the size of his neck; it resembled the circumference of a linebacker. "Don't know yet. Looks okay," he said hesitantly.

By now my heartbeat was in my throat, taking up residence. I'd started to sweat a little. Something felt off to me. I just couldn't put my finger on it.

"Ok, so what you got for me?" Raul glanced on both sides of himself. He was wearing a bulletproof vest. I could tell by the bulk. He pulled a grey backpack off his back and handed me a black Glock.

"Fully loaded. Here's the bullets." He handed over a small cardboard box and my trembling fingers retrieved it. My mouth felt like dry cotton. I tried to swallow, but my throat kept constricting, not wanting to work.

His square face furrowed into a frown. "You know how to use it?" He didn't have time to finish the sentence. I looked on in horror as two extremely muscular lean calves and thighs wrapped around his throat. Squeezing, I saw the muscles clench around Raul's large head. Raul gurgled from the anaconda-like grip as Raul's hands went to his throat to try and relieve the pressure. He tapped hard on the legs. I froze. I couldn't move. No words would come from my mouth. I watched the veins in his neck pop out and his eyes bulge bloodshot red. I didn't dare step out of the door to see the top half of the body. I knew it was that slimy, evil mother-fucker. The Viper. I clicked the magazine on the Glock in place and drew the slide back to chamber a round. Suddenly, the fight part of my response kicked in. Every single fiber in my body lit up like a Christmas tree as I got ready to pull the trigger.

A single mini dart pierced the skin of Raul's neck and the Viper's legs dangled as a slackened Raul fell to the paved asphalt outside my doorway. The Viper was riding on his back. I was still in partial shock, but I used the butt of my gun to hit out at the dangling legs. Bad move. I should have shot him. The Viper took advantage of my mistake and used the leverage of the door to swing in and kick the wind swiftly out of my chest, knocking me five feet backwards from the impact. I managed to hold onto the Glock with my dangling fingers.

"Fuck," I heaved. I landed inside the villa doors and felt

around my ribs, I wheezed from the impact as the Viper landed softly on his feet in front of me.

His eyes only held the essence of death and how to cause it. This time he was a redhead male, flaming orange – which is why I didn't pay much attention when I saw him near the café. I was focused on the wrong killer. But those glassy, soulless eyes were ones I would never forget. They haunted my dreams. I tumbled back, running into the edge of the table, wincing as the acute pain of being kicked took hold. Inside I was breaking, but I showed no fear. I pointed the gun straight at the Viper, my fingers quaking. "Don't move bitch, otherwise I'll shoot you!"

Darkness fell over the entire apartment as the Viper salivated and circled with his veiny hands hanging low beside his side.

"Howdy, li'l lady – we meet again. I must admit I liked the chase across the country. That was cute. Real cute," he said with a slow Texan drawl and greasy grin. Those yellow teeth made me want to vomit. His slack sallow skin glowing in the night. I swallowed the hard lump down in my throat. Sweat dripped down the back of my neck as my lip wobbled.

"I swear to fucking god. I will fucking shoot you," My weak, quivering tone was less than convincing. Even I didn't believe myself when I said it.

The Viper circled with his teeth bared and his slimy pink gums showing. I noticed his slippery feet closing the gap with his wiry legs. I stepped back, my throat on fire. I was on one side of the villa and he was on the other. I stumbled back into the kitchen counter and without thought I took a leaf out of Hawk's book and threw the steak knife at him. The Viper didn't even flinch, he ducked to the left and the knife rattled on the floor behind him. He was dressed in black as well. A beard with orange tinges throughout.

"Ha! You gotta do better than that. All this hullabaloo for nothing. Why don't cha just come with me, so we can get this over wit'?" The Texan accent made my lips curl with anger. The Viper closed the gap in a matter of a lightning second, my hands trembled so much I saw the Glock fall from my hands in slow motion. I bent to my knees to scramble and pick it up. The Viper scuttled across the table and launched at me like a tiger. I fell backwards on my head and hit the villa tile with a sickening thud. I tried to struggle momentarily as the weight of a thousand bricks landed on my chest. I knew my head had to be bleeding. The thud made my head pound with sound rushing through my ears.

I was out of time.

I'd failed.

I watched a rag cover my mouth as my world faded to black.

12

ELLIOT

In a perfect world, she would have stayed with me. In a perfect world, I would have rocked her body as many times as she could handle. I saw the images of me taking her up in a hot air balloon over Portugal. Us out to dinner, eating and enjoying the magic of one another. My walls came down with her in a way that I'd never experienced. Shocking and pure, the connection between us both. I was in love with the pretty investigator. Fucked up all my plans. Being in love with the enemy, now I had to find a way to lure her back to me. Even though I'd given her every last piece of me, she still refused. My heart ached for her sensual touch. Those bright sparkling eyes and her curious brilliant mind. I wanted to storm over and drag her back to my villa. I'd scribbled my Portugal number and a love heart on the paper on the way out. The chamber door to my heart was wide open. She was the only person who'd been able to unlock it. My cock still tingled to be inside of her, it wanted *only* her – which pissed me off. All the rest, if I bedded them, would be used as a release valve. Nothing more, nothing less.

A strange sound distracted me from my train of thought as I looked out of my villa window. What I saw made my stomach turn inside out. The view from my villa looked over the rooftops to Sara's row of villas. On top of the apricot-colored tiles was a man crouched down. He jumped down on top of another man and the man dropped like a ton of bricks on the pavement. I watched as I saw him swing off the door frame and into her villa. I didn't know what the fuck was happening, but I knew it was Sara's villa. I grabbed my gun from under my bed and ran blindly with it to her villa.

I didn't do this.

I was out of character.

I was a cool, calculated and ruthless man.

But all I saw was red, blazing in front of my eyes. I wasn't about to let anything happen to Sara. I couldn't. If we were playing the game, then okay – but not someone else. The oxygen debt was rapidly seeping into my legs as I ran slightly uphill to the back of the villas. Dust flew under my feet as the blood circulated. I looked down, avoiding the jagged uneven rocks under my bare feet. Her villa looked closer than it was from my window, but it was a good 900 yards away. I was scared I wasn't going to make it to her on time. Scared that whoever that deranged fucker was would have killed her. I sucked in the night air with my legs burning, which I didn't give two fucks about. I felt the tawny dirt of Portugal seeping in between my toes. Most of it was pure fine dirt, not gravel, so I ran smoothly with my legs pumping like pistons to her villa. My track sprinting was coming in handy now.

Most of the private villas were covered inconspicuously with palm trees, flowers and other plants. I made it with sweat dripping down the edges of my face. In front of the villa was a large man, I noted the glossy red bloodstain out front of her villa. I frowned. I swore I saw another man here... I moved inside, heart in my mouth looking around the villa. No sign of Sara anywhere. As I walked over to the kitchen, I noted the blood splashes. Fire burned in my soul. She was hurt! The son of a bitch hurt her. I followed the trail, eyes wild, searching, looking into the shadows of the kitchen light. The walkway lights from the villa allowed me to see. I tuned my ears so I could hear. I heard the distinct noise of dragging on the ground.

Where was it coming from?

The left or the right?

I jogged uphill to where the next villa was. I heard a car door slam. I looked up and a shiny black vehicle was parked with a man with orange hair dragging Sara into the vehicle. The headlights were on. The guy was a dummy. The car park was an abandoned section of the villa. It looked like it was for extension, that Piedre might have had the idea to build another villa. It was a separate area perched high and about 200 yards away from the others. I felt my emotions detach and ice run through my veins. I pulled my gun, cocked, squeezing off a shot, the 9mm parabellum bullet flying through the air, hitting the target's calf at 1500 feet per second.

"Fuckkk!!" The perp yelped in pain, buckling as he held his leg and dropping Sara as she slumped out of the car door. His breath was short winded as I saw him reach for his weapon. Vengeance was the only thing on my mind. *Too late.* My finger closed on the trigger and one clean shot fired to his temple through the violet midnight air. He slumped and fell away from Sara to the other side. I rushed to her with my heart almost bursting out of my chest and kicked the guy hard out of the way.

"Fuck Sara, take a breath for me," I said hoarsely. Her skin was cold and clammy, but she had a pulse. He'd drugged her. I knew what this was. I looked closely at the slime bucket. I shook my head. This looked like one of Clope's goons. I looked around to see if anybody heard what was going on. If Pierde heard the shots and saw them on camera, I would have to pay him off. No skin off my nose. He knew of my affiliations anyway. I pulled Sara's heavy limp body from the vehicle and gently laid her flat. I felt the back of her head as the warm crimson blood trickled onto my fingers. I winced and felt a hammer beat on my heart.

"Sara, come on baby, don't leave me. Wake up. This is my fault. Shit. Come on, fight back!" No response, but I felt the tiny beat in her wrist and under her neck.

I yanked my phone out of my pocket and rang Fabio "I need your help. Bring a cleanup crew Casa la Rosa. Top quarter," My request was straight to the point.

With his calm Columbian accent, he said. "Say no more. Call you when I arrive. Give me fifteen."

"'Kay, be quick."

"No problem." The phone clicked dead as I searched around the area for anything that might revive Sara, listening closely for her breath. I could feel the sweet warmness of her breath as I tried to kiss her back to life. The blood continued to leak from her pretty skull. The dead body of the guy who looked like a weasel was swimming in blood as narrow trickles seeped into the dirt. He received a nice clean round fleshy bullet hole in the middle of his head for his trouble. My attention went back to Sara. I ripped my shirt off and wrapped it around Sara's head working to stop the bleeding from the head wound. The rest of her body looked to be untouched. I prayed that nobody would find us. A strong wind came through, lifting the cinnamon dirt from the ground. I reasoned the other guests wouldn't need to come up here. My eyes ran over Sara's as I stroked her face. The part of my shirt I ripped off was soaked with bright red blood, I leaned over to check if she was still breathing. Either knocked out from the drugs or from concussion. My sole focus was the woman lying draped in my arms.

A lifetime passed, but eventually a squeal of tires swung up beside me, causing me to raise my arm from the film of dust cover. I recoiled as the dirt flicked up in my eye. Fabio rolled up in his black Mercedes van. I listened as his black boots crunched under him. He got out of the vehicle first with a toothpick in his mouth. Two other guys who looked like paramedics shot out of the vehicle. Both of them made a beeline for Sara and went to work on her. My clothes were drenched in her blood. I looked like shit, I knew. Fabio's olive-skinned face didn't bat an eye at the scene.

"How did you find me?" I asked quickly. On the outside I was calm but inside my heart pounded in my chest.

"Piedre. Camera," He nodded solemnly, giving me a puzzled look. I got up gingerly as the men attending to Sara lifted her onto a stretcher. I fixated on her as they patted some water on her face. My legs were wobbly and I steadied myself against Fabio's van. He pumped his hands palms downward to illustrate calm. "Don't worry, he's with us. Who do you think funds this place?" He arched his brows as I understood. "He's a good brother. What happened to the little lady?" Fabio leaned down and looked at her. "Pretty. She yours?" The two bulky men placed an oxygen mask on her and felt for a pulse.

My jaw tightened with territorial anger at Fabio's question. "Yeah, she is. Can you get her down to that villa right over there? She's got a pretty bad knock on her head."

One of them spoke, "Ok. We'll take care of it," as they carried her on the gurney to the villa.

"And who the fuck is that?" Fabio pointed with his ringed fingers to the assassin I'd once hired with his dark eyes. Appeared the goon wasn't satisfied with the full payment I gave him, despite not doing his job of taking Evana out in the first place.

"No fucking idea," I lied without directly looking at Fabio. The less he knew the better. He regarded me closely with a beat as a corrupt grin came over his face. He beckoned with two fingers to two other guys in the vehicle. Two heavy-set men in black with garbage bags and blankets rolled out of the back. They were wearing blue plastic gloves.

"Clean it up, guys. You know what to do," he said evenly. He slapped me on the back as I felt the tension lift. I rose up on my feet. Fabio let out a throaty chuckle, his leathery skin shimmering in the moonlight. He moved back from me and grabbed something from his vehicle.

"You look like shit, man. Not the billionaire I know. You must really love this one. Never seen you like this."

"You and me both," I sighed heavily. Fabio harpooned me a clean t-shirt.

I looked at it like a foreign object. "I keep it in the car for emergencies, you know."

"Cool." I stripped off the rest of my expensive linen shirt which was now badly tattered shirt off and tossed it onto the ground. I watched as Fabio lit up a cigar with his gold lighter.

"Claudio, light this for me," he said gruffly. The shadow of a man, with no sound, took what smelled like kerosene and poured it onto the shirt. Fabio took his lit match and dropped it onto the shirt, causing it to burst into flames.

He let out a creepy laugh. "Would ya look at that?" We both watched as the resplendent flames incinerated all evidence of my shirt. I knew what his goons would do with the bodies. I nodded my head as I shrugged into the black t-shirt he gave me. The body was packed into the vehicle while one of the men started the engine. Another poured a liquid that stung my nostrils on the ground.

Fabio steered me down the hill. "Let's go check on your girl." We walked with one another to the villa silently. That's the gangster code. Once the job is done, it's never spoken of again.

What murder?

What bodies?

I don't know what you're talking about.

The code that you live and die by. Another day at the

office, even in Portugal. The anger housed within was directed in different areas, one at myself for allowing Clope to hire this fool. The second at Ms. Clemens for her ravenous desire for justice. She just had to stick her nose in where it didn't belong. Lastly, mostly at myself for falling in love with a fucking investigator. Son of a fucking bitch.

We reached the villa and the two men who had worked on Sara stepped out.

"She's still asleep. He gave her a tranquilizer used on animals. She's going to be out for another few hours. We've stabilized the blood loss. She needed twelve stitches. It looked worse than what it was. Some bruising around the ribs, looks like she received some sort of blunt force trauma there. Her eyes are clear and it doesn't look like a brain injury that's life threatening. She's got a nice little knot for her trouble, though. If anything happens in the next few days take her to Garcia Hospital and ask for Dr. Andy Santos. He knows us. She might throw up a little but she will be okay," the guy said matter-of-factly in the dark.

"Thanks," I said grimly.

Fabio arched his heavy eyebrow at me. "You got it from here, camarada?"

"Obrigado. Yes." We dapped as the cleanup crew slung the black death van around with the door open. Fabio jumped in and the van drove off out of sight. I walked inside the place, as Sara slept peacefully on her back. She had a cream bandage bundled around her head. A smile crinkled from the corner of my lips. My little crusader. The paramedics had stripped her and taken the clothes. I saw them on the way out with the bundle. She was wrapped up in the villa blanket with two pillows behind her head. A tall glass of still water was next to the table, they'd placed it right in front of her along with some strong painkillers. I stroked her arm, and she moved slightly. The tension I didn't know I was holding dissipated.

How the fuck could I make it with her? I was used to being in control at all times. She nearly just died because of me. I was going to the heartland of hell after this life. I knew it. My eyes stung with what felt like tears. This one woman had brought me crashing to my knees. I moved a tendril of hair away from her face as she slept soundly. I sat like that with her for an hour, listening to her breathing. My hope was that she would wake up before I left and I would be the first person she saw in the morning. Her legs were on top of mine as I caressed them while she slept. So strong, but yet so feminine in her qualities. Her cute little button nose brought a smile to my lips.

I lifted her legs up after some time, moving to the counter. I saw her phone and the uncontrollable urge came over me to look through it. I knew it was locked, though, so I wouldn't be able to see much. But a clue.

As if I willed the phone to ring it did as it bounced on the dresser. I twisted my head back to Sara and she was still knocked out. I picked up the phone. A private number. Without thinking I answered.

"Hello?" Heavy breathing was on the other end of the line. "I said hello. This is Sara's phone."

"Uh, huh. Elliot." A male voice answered and the green-eyed monster of jealousy rose so violently in my soul I wanted to jump through the phone and rip the man's heart out.

"Who the fuck is this?"

"Your worst fucking nightmare. If you hurt her I will slice your throat open."

"Gotta get to me first, fucker. Who is this?"

"Trust me, you don't wanna know my name."

"Oh, but I do. You scared?" I spat back. The guy was cocky and calm.

"Not in the slightest. Always sending your goons to do

your dirty work. But one day I'm going to catch you on your own and you're going to beg for mercy," he affirmed.

The fury was about to fly from my lips, but by the time I formed a sentence the guy hung up. I looked at the phone. Damn, I couldn't unlock it. Ten missed calls. Seemed urgent. Who the fuck was this guy? I looked towards Sara with a hint of disgust. I would make her tell me. I looked at my watch. One hour 'til the meeting. I was cursing inside. I wanted to stay and nurse her back to health, but a potential growth of 300 million was on the line.

"Sorry baby. I can't stay." I padded softly over to her, kissing her pink-stained lips. "'Til we meet again." I had to find out who the fuck that guy was… and shut him down.

13

HAWK

W hen I arrived she was on her feet. I knocked on the door once.

"Who is it? Sara answered groggily.

"Hawk, open up," I said assertively. The villa was spectacular, clean, lots of warm reds and golds decorating the room. The villa doors were open on the other side as the Portuguese sun left a warm spotlight in the middle of the room. Sara had a bandage wrapped around her head, it hung low just above her eye.

I rushed to her as she wrapped her arms around my waist. "You okay?" I asked.

"I've seen better days," she sighed.

"What the fuck happened? I called you so many times and your fucking boyfriend picked up the phone." Her eyes were glassy, but she seemed alert. A note was on the table. I grabbed it and read it out loud. "Garcia hospital. Ask for Dr. Santos in the emergency ward if concussion worsens."

I watched as tears rolled down Sara's face. "It hurts. Elliot saved me. The Viper," she clutched her chest as I placed my hand on her shoulder.

"Sit, breathe for me, partner. We got this now. I should have got here sooner. I had to clean up in Istanbul," a pang of guilt hit my stomach that she was in so much pain and I couldn't reach her in time.

"I know Hawk. I know. I should have listened to you. To get the gun sooner. I don't remember the struggle. I can't– I can't remember. Shit." Both of her fists were balled up as she hit her thighs with them.

I sat beside her on the couch taking her hands. "Relax. Don't try to remember. I have most of the trail of events in my mind. I just want you to rest."

"This trip is fucked up, Hawk. So much for a holiday. Of course, only me," she bit out pitifully. Couldn't say I blamed her.

I stifled a laugh. "You know what you look like right now?"

"Shuddup. But tell me." She gave me a stink eye.

"You look like Humpty Dumpty that fell off the wall," I joked with a smile, trying to lift her spirits.

She laughed a little, and couldn't help it. "Don't make me laugh, Hawk. It hurts."

I became serious for a moment. "Do you know what happened to the Viper? Is it done? We can get into details later once you recover. I just want to know if I need to go on a recon mission."

"I don't know if he's dead. I presume so... Must be, because I'm here. I remember Elliot leaving out the door..." she trailed off.

I patted her leg. "We had a little chat. I tell you what: he's got it bad for you. He didn't like me on the phone," I added. Sara stared blankly at the wall. She wasn't telling me something. I could sense it with the way her eyes moved.

"Well that's Elliot. Does he know about you now?" Sara raised her eyebrows at me.

"Are you nuts? I'm practically a ghost. There's no way in hell that guy knows about me. He has no clue, and we are going to keep it that way."

"He knows I'm here, Hawk. He could come back any moment now, "she mentioned in a quiet tone.

"I'm aware, but I'm tracking him. I know his every move. He's connected to Miguel like I told you. So, any major moves he makes will likely mirror Elliot's. Miguel is harborside right now," I replied smoothly.

Sara stared at me. "Of course, you know where he is. Nicely done," she grimaced. I guessed from the headache.

"Let's not talk anymore. Rest up," I commanded.

Sara sat up rod straight. "Wait, security cameras, you… here. You can't be here."

"Relax. I knocked two of them in the security room. I put them on long loop replay. I also found the video with the Viper on it and Elliot. I have it here."

"How the hell..." Sara went to say, then just laid down in defeat.

"Let it go. Trust my methods. I might not have been here to stop it, but I have everything I need. You need to remember that Elliot saved you from a situation he caused. One that involved having you taken out," I warned as I felt the anger rise over the position he put her in.

"Elliot wouldn't hurt me... Not like that, anyway. If he wanted me six feet under, he would have done it by now." Her soft brown eyes stared wistfully at the black TV screen.

"I see what's going on here. No point lying to me. I have the tapes. Lucky for you. Stops Piedre from blackmailing you. You better hope he didn't make a copy. How do you know that Elliot didn't set you up and record you?" My eyes investigated hers as she became uncomfortable, fidgeting with her fingers.

"What the hell are you talking about, Hawk?" she said in a tired voice.

"You know exactly what I'm talking about. Take it easy. You need to rest. We can recap a little later."

Sara laid back, placing her hand over her head like a damsel in distress. "Urggh. This isn't the holiday that I dreamed of."

I got up and headed to the kitchen, sniffing around for food. I found what I was looking for inside the fridge. I pulled out the sandwich fillings of ham and cheese. I held up a glass jar to the light. "Hmm... chili chutney. Great. Just what an assassin needs," I mumbled. I made two sandwiches for both me and Sara and came back to the villa couch where she laid still.

"How are you feeling?"

She looked at me groggily. "I can't eat that right now. I will take some juice, though." She seized the orange juice from me and gulped it down. "Hmm. That's good."

I let a side eye fly and looked at her a little closer. A clear energy of guilt surrounded her – I could sense the lie in her. I stared at her face as she drained the orange liquid down. She gave me an absent-minded look. "What is it?"

"Have any regrets?" I posed.

Her forehead bunched together in the middle, then relaxed, her long lashes fluttering downward. "Like what? What would I regret?"

"Come on," I scoffed. "If Elliot knew you were here, I know for a fact he would have come for you." I shook the small tape reel I had in my hand. "Remember I have the tape in my hand. I'm about to load up my computer. The evidence doesn't lie."

She sat up slowly as I pulled my laptop out of my bag, along with my listening devices. I wanted to check in on Elliot's whereabouts now and see if I could get a read on the situation.

"Well, then let the evidence show what it does." She said with her earthy brown eyes looking back at me.

"Okay then," I muttered. I waited for the computer to load up. I felt the heat of Sara's gaze on me. I was sitting beside her with the wooden coffee table pulled forward. "Alright, show me what you got Elliot."

"I don't know anymore. I mean he hasn't been accused back home and we don't have the legal grounds to have him extradited. What's the point? He's just going to get away with it all," she proclaimed sullenly.

I glanced at her briefly as I logged into the mainframe, activating the tracking system online. She was slipping and I didn't blame her. Five red dots showed up in the same Portugal harborside location. Almada.

"Well, if an assassin tried to take me out and I got saved by the man I would feel the same as you... I mean, I would handle it a little differently." She eyeballed me with disdain. "Scratch that. Here we go. Five of them." I pointed to the computer screen, diverting her attention.

Sara, even in her recovery, seemed curious and sat up to take a look. "What does that mean, really? You're going to need more than that..." she added skeptically.

"You're right on the money there. But if I know who is in the game, then I can start reeling them in like fish. This tracking device traces the phones."

"How did you do that?" I heard the faint clog of the wheels start turning in Ms. Clemens brain.

"Feeling better?" I observed with a small chuckle.

"Sort of. Anyway, this is helping – so keep going." She perked up just a little.

"When Miguel called and I tracked him in Istanbul, he rang Elliot. I was able to trace it back to what looks to be his Portuguese number. I've been honed in on him ever since. Now whatever calls he makes I will be able to trace and see who he's in cahoots with." I tapped Sara's leg lightly, thrilled with my discovery. I picked up my sandwich without looking and bit into it.

"Once this tracks the phone, it tracks the person, too, and provides directions. Pretty cool, courtesy of the US Homeland Security network." I felt a piece of cheese falling out of my sandwich. I chased the cheese that landed on Sara's thigh. I picked it off and put it on my tongue for consumption.

She kicked out at me slightly. "Slob."

"You're supposed to be resting. I did you a favor. I didn't want slops landing on you."

"Why thank you, Hawk. I appreciate it," she said sarcastically.

"I personally think the only way this case is going to blow open wide is if Clope gets convicted. From what Dermas told me, that's not looking so good."

Hawk arched a brow. "When did you talk to Dermas again?"

"I spoke to him on the day I left. He came to help me with the window situation with the Viper. It doesn't matter – the guy is dead now," she said.

"He followed you from the restaurant. You were an easy target. I would say you have your answer. He was in your house. You weren't going crazy. I think you should get that window sweeped regardless to confirm. Piece of mind."

"I agree. I'm going to lay down now and not talk for a while," she said softly.

"Wait a minute. Wait a minute. Let me check your pupils." Ever since our first run in together, I'd always been protective over Sara. For the life of me I couldn't figure out why, so I didn't try anymore. I just shielded her. I reached around in my laptop bag and pulled out a small flashlight.

"You have everything in there," she said as she sunk back into the couch.

"I have a few tricks up my sleeve." I pressed the light, opening her lids wide.

"I'm right here. I can open my own eyes," she flipped me away with her hand.

"I just need to get a closer look. Do you feel dizzy? If we need to get you to the hospital to check I'm happy to take you," I said softly.

"No. Go ahead and look, Hawk." I waited 'til she laid back and opened her eyes. I pulled downward gently on her lower lids and looked inside. Her pupils looked good. Her breathing was steady, her blinking in rhythm. Concussion was one of those things to watch carefully.

"I've already been asleep and napped," she added.

"I'll be here anyway, so if I see anything we are taking you straight to the hospital." I let her know firmly what the deal was.

"I don't want you to blow your cover," she reasoned.

"I'm a spy, Sara. I know how to not be seen if I need to."

"Well okay then, Mr. Spy." She turned on her side on the couch and I lifted a blanket over her. I went back to my sandwich and continued to track Elliot's course. They were still in the same spot. I wanted to pick up the other names at the table. I hoped the phones were all in close enough vicinity that I could pick up their signals and identify the players.

I touch screened the red dots, so I could pull up the details individually. Each one popped out. Miguel Herrera I already knew. I pressed on the second red dot. A phone number appeared. I winced in frustration. This is where I needed two computers, but I would have to make do. "+315... Hmmm, let's see... Who the hell are you involved with?" I said out loud.

I ran the number through my database. Donte Guzman. Mexican in his sixties, a rap sheet a mile long. Drug trafficking charges, served five years in La Mesa in the early 90's. I chuckled to myself. La Mesa was no different than what I imagined Donte's outside world to be. Donte would have had a field day in there. La Mesa State Penitentiary was a gang-run prison where prisoners paid for their cells and lived like drug kingpins. The drug hustle on the inside of La Mesa took on a life of its own, and I'd heard the legendary stories. The prison guards were weak and bribed well enough to keep quiet, plus the government worked together with the jail. I took another bite of my sandwich and swallowed down some juice. Donte didn't *really* go to jail because La Mesa became housing for the poor people of Mexico.

Elliot, who the fuck are you dealing with?

I typed in Donte's name. He became a local hero in Mexico, owning over 70% of Tijuana's real estate. My mind came to the measured conclusion, easy for him to make trap houses when you owned them. The pieces were coming together. Thirty minutes in, I looked around to Sara on the couch, tucked in the fetal position. She stirred. A light snore which made me smile slightly.

I pulled up the next red dot on the screen attached to the local number. "Hmm... Fabio. What a name," I muttered under my breath. I finished my orange juice as the Portuguese sun changed its location, now shining on my computer screen. *"Shit."* I picked up my gear and relocated to the kitchen table.

I resumed my studies. Fabio Coron Vazquez, a Columbian. Also middle aged, late fifties. I looked calmly through the records. Shady connections to the Pistoleros, no records, which made me raise both my eyebrows. So, the guy had a great cover. Job Occupation, distillery merchant. Address Cucata. I pulled up his location: *of course,* a sprawling million-dollar mansion. My mind drew it all together.

Columbia, Portugal, America, Mexico – and I hadn't finished with the other two. They were forming a world-wide drug network with the heavy hitters. I let my eyes settle for a moment and got up to stretch my legs. I pulled the heavy-duty burgundy curtains back, looking out over the Tagus River. I reveled in the natural light flooding through the villa apartment. I'd spent about an hour looking into them. As I did, Sara woke up, stretching out her legs and lifting herself up from the couch. She rubbed her eyes sleepily.

"Arrghh. I'm going to wash my face. I wanna hear what you found out," she said in heavy slumber.

"How's your head?" I questioned as she touched the side of her bandage.

"I'm okay. The lump is still there. I probably look like an alien. But I'm alive, that's the main thing."

"Right. Do you have more bandages? I want to check the wound and make sure it heals properly," I commanded.

"Are you a doctor, too?" I rolled my eyes at her. "Yes, they left a bunch in the corner near the entrance. Looks like an ice pack, too. I'm going to use that. I don't want an egghead."

"Ok. Given your taste in men I would say you need a doctor," I concluded.

"Low blow, and while I'm not at my best." Sara replied coolly.

"Best time to strike. Take it easy," I said softly as she walked gingerly to the bathroom.

"I will. You can look at it. It's no problem."

"Ok, good." I went back to the computer and continued pinpointing the team. A South American number. I retrieved the name. Juan Galvez, Peruvian background. The dude looked like a player. I ran his name through the database. Sure enough. Drug trafficking. *This slick bastard.* Elliot thought himself invincible. I checked the screen; it didn't look like anyone else had shown up. I slapped the table. If I had a wiretap on the phone I could hear the conversation.

Sara came out of the bathroom with a shocked look on her face. "What happened?"

"Nothing. I need a wiretap right now. I know what Elliot's doing here." Sara moved the hair from her face as I watched her walk. She was at least walking straight. "Sit. Want a hot or cold drink?"

"Well, if I'm going to be dizzy like this, how about a G & T," she joked with a lopsided grin. Good to see her grinning, but she wasn't out of the woods yet.

"What's funny?" she said as I held in a laugh at her bandage job.

"You are. Your bandage is lopsided and hanging over your eye. Take a seat and let me take a look at the wound. Make sure it's not infected." Sara sat down in front of me as I grabbed a bowl and placed tepid water in it. I yanked the tea towel off the rack as I came back to the table. She sat silent as the light streamed onto her.

"How's Evana?" She queried.

"She's good. Couldn't make it. Her shoot is running over. But we're solid. She's not a bad little informant either," I confirmed.

"I don't even want to know, Hawk. I don't." I unraveled the crepe bandage around her head, noting the crimson blood stains spotted on them as I got close to the end of the wrap. The wound was sealed tight with a neat row of navy-blue stitches. A lump the size of a tennis ball made up the wound with a little caked-up blood. I dabbed the cloth in the water and dabbed slowly across the wound, removing the caked-up residue.

"Is that okay?" I enquired about the temperature of the rag.

"Yes. Completely fine. How is it back there?"

"Nothing major, just a small little knot," I lied.

"Hawk, you are lying. I can feel it. She placed her hand on the back of her head and gasped sharply. "*I knew it!* It's huge. I need to put ice on it. Oh my god. I'm a mess."

"It will be fine. Just thank your lucky stars you weren't chopped into little pieces. Could be a lot worse," I reminded her.

She shuddered, covering her arms. "Could have been way worse. I'm so grateful it wasn't."

"Hey. You're okay now. I have some good news. If we can piece this together, we can get this intel across to the US Homeland Security Network to track Elliot. I just need a little more to make it happen. I already took down the head of the arms trafficking network in Istanbul so Miguel will be fuming. I'm surprised he's attending this meeting." I removed the packaging and applied a new bandage around Sara's head, wrapping it carefully.

"Which one was it. My memory…"

"No surprises there… about your memory. Miguel Herrera, the local. His new arms leader is dead. He was there for the shooting."

"You didn't see his reaction?" I pinned the bandage in place, happy with my handiwork. I handed Sara a snap freeze ice pack to bring the swelling down.

"No. I don't hang around with a bag of popcorn for the show," I replied smugly.

She ignored my sarcasm. "Tell me what's going on, Hawk?"

I breathed out a sigh. "Elliot is working on an international smuggling and drug network and expansion into New York ports."

14

ELLIOT

☖

She's what I didn't know I wanted. She's what I didn't understand I needed. Everything that was never part of my life.

Love.

This suffocating, piercing ache inside my chest. An ache that threatened to cloud my sharp judgement. I'd already been caught with my pants down. *Literally.* I drew in air as I reminisced about the taste of her lips. Her sultry moans as I explored every delicate curve of her body. She'd been worth waiting for. Problem was I was addicted, I wanted more of her, I wanted her to see the other sides of life. I'd grown bored of the usual bimbos I met. Ms. Clemens was exciting; she amplified every feeling within me. No matter what, I vowed to see her again before she left. I set my mind to it.

I was harborside, overlooking the azure waters of the Tagus River. The café I sat at was drenched in sunshine yellow. Yellow umbrellas with matching striped yellow and white tablecloths, and a plethora of people enjoying the seaside. Some had just disembarked from the nearby ferry.

The sky was lined with nothing but pale blue, not a cloud in sight. I sipped my milky latté as I waited for the others. Large cargo boats crossed the river silently with the tugboat chugging alongside them. Soon my drug shipments would be crossing over to the United States with my product on them. I inhaled the mild sea breeze as the sea gulls squawked, landing beside me on the nearby railing. I really was on top of my game. No longer did I feel like I was in my father's shadow.

My father has always been a competitive man. I remembered what he said on my 21st birthday;

"Don't disgrace me in life, son. Make me proud. But know this: there's only one big dog in the family. Until you can prove you are one, you won't get all the keys to the castle. Happy 21st, your car's outside." Then he'd kissed the top of my head and handed me the keys to a Porsche 911. One of the more confusing traits of my father. You never knew if you were in trouble or if he was showing love.

I let the salty air whip my tousled hair around as I sipped and waited. I wanted to check in on Sara. I frowned a little as I peered into the Portuguese crowd. I had to do something about Piedre… Feel out the situation. I wasn't a man to leave strings untied. We'd had good dealings for years and he didn't ask any questions, so I figured it would all turn out well. Now, the news of Fabio being in building was interesting. Could use it to my advantage down the line. Chairs were perched on the rocky edge with the water lapping right at the bottom of the barnacle-covered rocks.

My flagrant thoughts were interrupted by Miguel. His olive face was loaded with tension as the cool, calm waters of the man I met at first now resembled a tsunami.

"Hey, Miguel," I greeted him cordially, holding out my hand for a customary handshake.

"Robert, nice to see you again. Great choice of place," he nodded with respect.

"Thanks. I've always found the water to be very soothing. Don't you agree, Miguel?" His movements were skittish. I let my icy eyes land on him.

"Very much so." Miguel was dressed conservatively in khaki pants, a blue long sleeve top and a light taupe jacket. If you looked for him in a crowd, you would miss him.

"You look as if you have something on your mind, my friend. Care to share?" I probed as he sat down with his tight eyes and furrowed brow.

"Let me get a drink first and something to eat." Something had thrown him off balance. He lifted one finger to the waiter, who came quickly.

"Ginjinha for both of us. We have others coming as well." Miguel looked to me for approval. "Robert, let's share a seafood platter."

"Agreed. I like the sound of it," I replied. The waiter nodded and went away.

Miguel raked his well-weathered hand through his hair. "It's been a rough few days."

"Sorry to hear," my reply, deadpan. I didn't trust this man. *Not one fucking bit.* My pale eyes were fixed on him, waiting to hear what had him shaken, which I, in fact, already knew about. I didn't need any dead weight on my team.

"Nothing I can't sort out and nothing that will impact our operation," he said quickly averting his eyes to the sea.

I arched a brow at him. "You mean the arms trafficking ring you failed to mention to me, Miguel?" I dropped the bombshell. Ricardo had been a man of his word. A cherry red substance in a small shot glass came to the table. Miguel's eyes held savagery. Seemed misplaced to me as I was the one he tried to omit the information from and double cross. A wry twisted smile came over my face. I knew how to draw my opponents out into the open.

"Did you have something to do with his death?" he asked.

Confused, I looked at him. *Wrong response, and what was he talking about?*

"Well on that note, I don't know what you're referring to… But as far as finding out about the guns, I have my sources." Miguel's olive face looked as if it might burst into flames.

"I oughta turn this fucking table over and shoot you at point blank range," he countered, his jowls shaking.

I sat calmly as I eyed the cherry red liquid. One of my favorite liqueurs from Portugal.

"But you won't. I actually wanted to strike a 50/50 deal with you. Not my line of exact business, but I know some network who would be very interested. For a fair price, of course. You didn't really think you would smuggle the extra gun shipments for free and without me knowing, did you?" I studied Miguel as the subtly cherry-flavored liquid ran down my throat. Miguel followed suit.

"No. I planned to tell you. I thought since I was working on the immigration side of things, to keep you out of trouble with Interpol, you would be okay," he retorted.

I narrowed my eyes sharply at Miguel. I bared my teeth like a wolf. "You thought wrong. They don't have anything on me. *At all.* They are asking me to come back for questioning. But they have no ability to bring me back to the States. *None.* So, let's work out a deal. Put a figure on the napkin, and I'm sure we can work something out." I paused, taking in his red face. "I'm not one to stop a man's enterprising nature. In fact, I applaud it." My fingertips touched in a triangle as I watched for any sharp movements. Miguel's Adam's apple bobbed up and down and the anger in his eyes didn't extinguish.

"So, you had nothing to do with any hits?" he asked fervently.

"No, I didn't, but sounds like you got yourself into some trouble. I don't have any reason to conduct a hit. I'm trying to do business with you, remember? Doesn't serve my purpose or yours," I said coolly.

Miguel's body weight shifted away from me as his silent but deadly eyes finally released their heat. "Yes. I suppose it wouldn't make sense. Again, I planned to tell you. I wanted to come to the table with my ducks in a row." I saw his nose twitching. I could tell he was lying. He never planned to tell me. *He planned on me never finding out.* I let him run with it. He was falling right into my hands.

"So, as I said. Write the number down on the napkin and we can adjust. I will get in touch with my buyer. Help you expand that network. You obviously have contacts. I presume them to be military?"

"Yes. Through Mexican borders," he declared.

"I see. Well, my networks in that niche are closer to the Canadian border."

"Ah huh. How about this?" Miguel moistened his chapped lips and pulled a Parker pen from his top pocket. The number he wrote had a few zeroes in it. I nodded.

"Not a bad first offer. I was thinking something more like this." I up leveled by another three million. I really didn't care; it was more of an ego-tripping exercise of a man who dared double cross me.

Miguel settled down as three of the other men arrived together at the table. Miguel confirmed with a nod. "Okay. But if I find out you had anything to do with the murder of Prince Saeed, I will personally chop your balls off," he hissed in a low voice.

"Fine by me. But I can assure you, unless it affects my business, I don't order unnecessary hits. Not my style," I smiled slyly at him. Besides, of late my hitmen had been unreliable. Interesting to know he just revealed the information I needed. Now Miguel was exposed. I let the breeze hit my nostrils; I would have my informants regulate the situation.

Sounded like Middle Eastern connects. My gut feeling never lead me astray. Miguel *was* the man to watch.

"Elliot and Miguel. The early birds to the table. Olá amiga!" Juan announced his entrance with flamboyance and Peruvian charm. I broke into a shit-eating grin as he greeted me with a hug, especially since I just made more money. Juan wasn't one to be ignored. He wore a cream silk patterned shirt and tight black shorts with loafers. I got up to receive the hug. Fabio and Donte greeted us and found their seats.

Donte was dressed head to toe in white, his cologne strong and burning my nose hairs as he took up residence next to me.

"Gentleman. Today is a celebration. We are carving our new lane. We are about to become incredibly rich. Is everyone ready with their respective inputs?" Donte rubbed his hands together.

In unison everybody nodded. I felt the heat from Miguel's eyes, but he knew he had nowhere to go. I knew to have my watchdogs on standby in case he tried anything. I wasn't a man for complacency. Donte looked around and said, "I'll call the waitress, we are going to feast: eat, drink, be merry and talk business. How about it, Roberto?"

I flashed a big grin. When it was time to play I was all chips on the table. "Sounds good. We got a seafood platter coming. How about we get a few more?"

Donte squeezed my shoulder "Done, minha amiga." He called the waitress and placed an order for drinks and more seafood. The waitress came out with the first platter. Plump orange prawns fully shelled arrived at the table along with mussels, oysters, salmon, fresh calamari and shoestring fries. Three bottles of white wine and more Ginjiha came as well. The splash of crisp wheat-colored wine hit my glass as the waitress poured. Everyone was in high spirits, except for Miguel who snuck death daggers at me as he looked over at me. I would need to keep an eye on him – that's for sure.

Donte clicked his silver teaspoon against his wine glass making me jump out of my fog.

"Gentlemen, now that we've had a couple of drinks under our belt and we're enjoying this Portuguese weather and its people, let's get started. We're going to roll around the table and every man can say his piece. I have tentative dates for shipment roll out in 30 days based on what happens here today at this meeting. We have ourselves a new brotherhood. Let's toast to that Familia." I held my glass high in the air with the others clinking. At the head of the table was Fabio. No mention was made about the rescue or murder. *That's the code.* Fabio, in his tan leather jacket, shrugged out of it.

"We worked out your little problem, Elliot, with the Columbians. They owe us a favor so they are letting that payment slide." He held up his wine glass. "I explained the situation on your behalf, and that it was out of your hands. We negotiated a deal that set it straight. They owe us anyway and agreed," Fabio explained.

"Hell yeah to that." I guzzled down more of my wine.

Fabio smiled and continued. "Now we are the owners of the main coca producers set up across Columbia. We have shipments ready to go." Fabio saluted and bit the head off his prawn with force.

"How much product are you able to move?" Donte asked.

"Let's start with 10,000 pounds. Let's start small and then work steadily. Best way to do it. Stay steady. We will run the container ship from Columbia through to Mexico, then switch – right Robert? – to your cargo?"

"Yes. That's right, nice and smooth. Set the dates and I will make the calls to the yard to set things in place."

"So, we measure everything correctly and in case of any situations we will work backwards and send another 10,000 pounds through Portuguese ports and then through your waters, Miguel."

Miguel nodded as he stabbed a piece of calamari with his

fork. "Yes, works fine by me. I need two weeks' notice to make the arrangements. I have all the port authorities on payroll. They are aware. Should be a nice, easy transaction," he said gloomy.

Donte cleared his throat and a devious sparkle dominated his eyes. "This is just the beginning. The location is the same. United States. We will stagger the shipments and ports. I will manage the ports of Mexico. No problem at my end. I just need a week's notice. Juan, what does your product look like?"

"Same as Fabio. We will run through to him from Peru. We have new coca regions and we are friends with the police. They don't check our regions. The product is smooth. Incredible quality," he said cheerfully. Nice guy. I liked him.

"Looks like I'm going to need to expand my distribution network," I reasoned with a cagey smile.

Donte's rich laughter filled the air. "Looks like it, Robert. Now let's eat and talk some more."

15

SARA

 few days later, early morning texts rained in from Elliot...

WHO WAS the guy on the phone?
   Who the hell is this?
   Elliot
   How do you have this number?
   I have my ways. Answer the question.
   One of my other lovers. I smiled and no response came through for another ten minutes.
   Liar. How is your head, baby?
   Feeling better
   Good. I want to see you
   I told you no. I'm cutting off this number.
   I will come to you so no difference.
   "Dammit Elliot!" I stomped my foot. I was standing in the middle of the villa and wishing I didn't just make the costly, but most erotic mistake of my life by sleeping with Elliot. The impulsive imp inside me had won out this time. I closed my

eyes, breathing in and out for a few. He must have gotten the number while I was resting. My head throbbed for another few days, but at least I was able to take the bandages off. Alive because of Elliot, and on the other hand given a death sentence because of the hit he put out. This man's presence in my life had made my existence a ball of mass confusion. Given what Hawk told me about Elliot expanding his operation, you would think I was focused on that. All that poured into my mind was Elliot sliding down my turned-on body with those magic lips hitting all my sensory spots.

Every time I attempted to focus on researching the men from Elliot's camp and to contact Interpol, it's all I recollected. If I wanted to gain more insight into his operation it would be better to get closer to him, I justified to myself. My pussy tingled at the thought. Only I knew deep in my gut that I didn't know if I had enough emotional separation from Elliot.

You know you want to... You can do it. You can play both sides. It won't hurt. Just get what you need and bounce. The imp was chattering, and I wanted it to shut up. That type of coercion wasn't needed right now. I touched the back of my head as the sun shone through my villa, the light hitting some of the exquisite ornaments. Only a small lump that I could slide my fingers back and forth over now. Lucky for me my ebony locks covered it. I felt a lot better after a lot of rest, watching movies and sitting in the bath soaking. My ribcage was nearly back to normal from the kick the Viper inflicted. Most of my memory didn't come back after the kick to the stomach, for which I was glad.

I opted to sport a cute sundress and leather sandals. I wanted the sunshine to kiss my face and *not* to be studying a case I didn't think I could win for several reasons. As I reached for my handbag, a vision flashed of the Viper flying at me. I inhaled a sharp breath and said out loud, *"It's over now, Sara. He can't touch you. He's dead."* Still, the image of a slimy evil face was so vivid. I locked the villa door behind myself. My fingers were crossed for a nice, simple, normal day. As I walked to the bottom of the reception area, I noticed the happy couples and people roaming in and out. Their energy was infectious and I began to feel my holiday wasn't lost altogether. I called Donovan. I figured he would know the best places to take me.

"Donovan, are you free? I would love a little tour of the city. I know it's short notice. If–"

He interjected. "No madam, please. It would be my pleasure."

"Brilliant," I beamed, finally feeling *some* hope. As I spoke to Donovan, I felt the wind change as I looked out at the villa palms, their green spikes blowing back and forth effortlessly. Elliot with his sexy pale blue eyes snatched the phone from my slender hand as my mouth hung open in shock.

"She won't be needing you today, but thank you anyway. Appreciate it." Elliot with one hand casually in his chino shorts pocket pressed the end call button, handing the phone back to me. I wanted to frown but it was as if I'd just had Botox and the frown wouldn't form.

"What the hell are you doing?"

Elliot's face lit up, making my heart melt into goop. "I'm taking you on an adventure today. Come with me, Sara. I want to make it up to you. I want to show you what we could be. Be with me today." The earnestness in his voice, his sublime presence, was too hard for me to resist. I just stared into his chest for a moment. He tipped my chin up to meet his smoldering gaze. I listened to the splashes in the pool behind us as a black town car arrived at the front.

I knew the decision I was about to make would forever change my destiny. Elliot held out his arm. "Sara, *just let go.* Come with me." His ocean blue eyes met mine as if we were walking along the ocean for the first time together. I saw my legs floating to the sleek town car; it was like having an out of body experience. I watched myself glide onto the seat. I let go of the air holding time in my lungs. I must have stopped breathing for a moment. Elliot slid in beside me comfortably, our knees touching on the plush velour seats. He interlocked his fingers with mine seamlessly. I closed my eyes for a minute, opening them to Elliot's intrusive gaze. I saw the driver wave as I gave him a timid wave back.

"What are you thinking? You haven't said anything, my love." He brought my hand to his lips and kissed it so tenderly it made me want to cry.

"I don't know what to say. What is there to say? I can't stay away from you." I shrugged my shoulders.

"Say how you feel. *Tell me*. I want to know," Elliot asked gently. Elliot tapped the front glass to alert the driver. "Go to Coruche. You know where."

"I'm mixed up, to be honest," I lamented. Elliot pulled two chilled glasses out from the fridge.

"Champagne. I think this is a celebration."

I ran my hands through my hair, pulling at the ends. "Okay, I'll have one glass." He smirked at me.

"What?"

"It's not my plan to get you drunk, Ms. Clemens. I have a little more class than that. Besides, it's not something I need to do. I don't want anything to be forced."

"You practically took the phone out of my hand just now. I was just fine until you came along." Elliot handed me the chilled glass and it somewhat broke the dark spell. The drive was smooth, though I had no idea where we were going.

"Well, we needed a little intervention. You and I are similar whether you know it or not. We go after what we want. You're headstrong, so am I. I want to be with someone who can challenge me. Keep me on my toes at times. Plus, I fucked up."

I licked my lips as I eyed his. I quickly sipped my drink so as to stop myself from kissing him. "Elliot you tried to have your ex-wife killed and you saved me from that fucking assassin *you* hired. You created the mess. You have criminal dealings and I'm an investigator. This is all kinds of wrong... How can you not see that?" I said with tempered frustration. I drank a little more as the bubbles flowed through my wired system. Made me feel a little light, but better. I watched as we crossed the Tagus River.

Elliot breathed deep. "This is my fault." He circled my leg lightly with his finger. "I should have pursued you at the beginning." I turned to him, not in shock because now the dance we did seemed to be normal. "We have some things to sort through. *Sure*. We can do it. My feelings for you are not a game. I don't make a habit of sleeping with the enemy – not knowingly, anyway," he added with a sardonic smile.

"Then tell me what this looks like to you? Besides, I'm not trying to kill anyone," I asked with fire searing in my eyes.

He just stroked my hand and ran his fingers along my skin with excruciating slowness. Goosebumps formed and the response brought a wicked smile to his lips. "You look beautiful today, radiant as ever in your sundress."

"Don't try and change the subject, Elliot," I responded swiftly.

"It looks like a day where we let the troubles of this modern-day world pass us by. Where you let me make up to you what happened."

"I wish I had my tape recorder. You just admitted ordering a hit."

Elliot laughed out loud. "You know that's not going to stand up in court, baby. C'mon."

"Still you would be watched," I tried to redeem myself.

"I'm always being watched. Nothing new," Elliot posed. "Now stop fighting me and get over here, where you belong." In the most intimate of embraces Elliot slid his arm around my back, his spicy cologne seducing me into delicate surrender. The other caressed my thigh, sending a hot current raging through me. His darkened eyes softened as his lips deftly opened mine. A low primal moan rose from Elliot. "What you do to me is nothing short of incredible, Ms. Clemens." His silky huskiness turned me all the way on and I wanted him to take me right in the backseat. The realization of the driver having a feast in front of his eyes, stopped me.

"I like it when you call me 'Ms. Clemens'," I whispered seductively. He nibbled at my bottom lip.

"There she is. My hot little minx. I knew you were in there," Elliot sweet talked. Our tongues melded; a desperate urgency governed by time constraints. I cupped his face with my long fingers, letting them linger on his two-o clock shadow. I enjoyed the moment, drinking in his masculine energy. When I looked in his cool blue eyes I didn't see darkness anymore, I saw a calm sea. I saw a man tormented by a life built for him. Set out before him without freedom of choice. He closed his eyes as our connection deepened. I felt as if it was just me and him. As the car moved along its path, it seemed the problems we had didn't exist. I sipped the rest of my champagne and so did Robert. If only for this one fleeting moment we could be together. I let the butterflies in my stomach carry me away.

After some time, I asked, "Where are we going, Robert?"

"Somewhere beautiful. You're going to love it. I guarantee you, it will be a whole lotta fun." His cheeky smile made me ease back into my seat. I believed him. I felt alive – Elliot made me feel like that. Minutes later, I felt the town car ease to a stop near a grassy area with the citrine sun rising over Portugal. We were in the countryside surrounded by sap green and golden flecked fields everywhere as I stepped out of the car and into fresh, crisp air. The refreshing Portugal morning topped up my lungs as I stretched my arms wide. No breeze, just country air and perfect stillness. The sky was tinted in candy pink and splashed with slivers of violet. Fluffy pearl-colored clouds littered the back half of the sky. In front of us was a large basket with a brightly-colored parachuted balloon and strings holding it to the ground. A bald-headed man was in front grinning from ear to ear. Another younger man was securing the ropes and double-checking beside him.

I gasped. "A hot air balloon. *Wow.* I've never been in one of these," I exclaimed.

Elliot's face opened up into a boyish grin. "Told you. I knew you would love it."

"You're right, this isn't what I had in mind," I answered, mesmerized.

Elliot tapped the car as the driver rolled his window down. "Pick you up around three boss, right?"

"Yes, Ricardo. See you then." He winked as they shared a knowing. An insecurity swept in my mind as I faced Elliot.

"You've brought women here before, I assume?"

"No. I've brought my friends here, but never someone I care about." Robert held out his hand with a heartfelt smile and a solemnness that had me believe him. I took it, and the warmth radiating from him sent heat up my spine.

"Okay. I'll buy that for now."

He threw back his head in laughter. "I expected nothing less from you."

The jolly old man with a protruding stomach, olive skin and white wispy hair smiled so hard it made his eyes crinkle in the corners. "Hello, Elliot. Good to see you again. And who is the lovely lady you're here with?"

Elliot squeezed my hand. "Sara, and yes – she is lovely." He lifted my fingers to his mouth and kissed my hand. I felt the heat flush across my cheeks. He really did know how to cater to a woman. I would give him that.

Enjoy the moment, Sara. Just enjoy it. Even if it's not real.

"Hi. Nice to meet you. And your name is?" I asked as I held out my hand to the man. His fat rounded fingers enveloped mine.

"Gus is my name. I'm from Lisbon and have been taking

people across the skies of Coruche for the last twenty years. Today we are going to experience Lisbon hot air balloon style," he relayed flamboyantly.

"Ooo, sounds good," I said with excitement, clapping my hands.

Robert grinned at me. He seemed so happy, not a face I often saw from him. It changed his whole demeanor. Elliot and I stepped into the hot air balloon as Gus relayed a set of instructions to us. As the hot air balloon rose to the sky, the world changed before my eyes. I looked down watching the ground beneath us move. I gazed out over the great expanse of fields; it made me realize how small we were as humans. I heard the faintness of Gus's narration in the background, along with the gas from the hot air balloon, but I wasn't exactly listening.

To the left is River Sorraia which leads into the famous Tagus River...

I let the beauty of silence between us linger as I admired the beauty of Portugal's countryside. A peaceful indigo river to my left and a sea of green blocks of land separated by dusty roads. Woody trees lined the fields swaying with the breeze. Gus's voice eventually broke through to me as Elliot watched me. I was thankful he was giving me space to take in the beauty of all that was.

"Would you like a ham and cheese croissant? I also have some tea and coffee here." Gus held up two Thermoses. A few things made me surprised: one of them was Elliot's choice of adventure and the simple things that brought a smile to his face.

"Yes, to both, and I'll take the tea." I smiled as I pointed to the silver Thermos.

I gave Elliot a lingering look as he leaned to kiss my cheek. "What is it?"

"Nothing. I really like this. I just thought of you as..."

Elliot seemed amused as I admired the dimple flowering on his cheek. "You thought what, Ms. Clemens?"

I turned slightly away from him. "I thought you might like different things than this. I always imagined you to be into fast cars and adrenaline-based activities."

Elliot arched both his brows at me. "Then you underestimated me. I'm a well-rounded human. That's why I wanted you to spend time with me. Now you know who I really am." He swept an arm around me dragging me into his arms as Gus poured the tea for us both. "I'm not quite the monster you think," his husky voice in my ear, giving it a nip.

"Well, monsters hide well, don't they?" My eyes sparkled back at him as I slid my index finger down the edge of his well-cut jaw. He bit it playfully as I recoiled from the ticklishness.

Gus handed us both our cups of tea and two plastic plates with ham and cheese croissants on them. The next sight made me gasp in delight. A cluster of whitewashed houses and villas with their apricot hats appeared below, along with many churches.

"Ah yes. Beautiful isn't it? Coruche, a peaceful village town."

"Gus, all the houses are white! Reminds me of Greece," I said.

Gus nodded. "Yes, it's quite fascinating. Part of the architecture and the times. White was used to reflect the heat and keep houses cool in summer. Coruche is known as the Town of Cork as it's surrounded by cork trees. The ones you just saw over the countryside." Gus pointed out. "This is what the town is known for, along with our crops these days. We have very rich soil and the river that runs through."

I nodded as I finished my ham and cheese croissant. "What a different world. Thank you, Gus."

"My pleasure. Elliot, are you living in Almada now, my

friend?" Gus asked. I let a forced smile cross my lips. It seemed like everywhere we went, Elliot knew everybody.

"Yes, I'm in the same villa. I'm thinking to buy it." I finished my tea as the township of Coruche sailed by.

"Of course," I responded smugly. *What didn't the man own?*

"I own a lot of things, Sara, but not all the things I want." The taunting tease in his voice made me cross my arms. It was obvious I was next on the list of 'things to claim.' Gus let out a hearty chuckle.

"Ah, my dear friend, the heart is not to be owned. It is to be treasured and set free." He patted Elliot on the shoulder as he packed the empty mugs away. "I should know, I've been married thirty-five years," Gus mumbled. I smiled. Finally, a man who understood.

"I'm beginning to find that out, Gus." Elliot spoke in my direction as I stared back at him, blank faced. A luscious green field came into view up ahead to take my attention away.

"We have been in the air for about forty-five minutes. We have a nice field coming up, this will be our place to land. You can see a few other ballooners out today." He pointed to the multicolored balloons in the sky. I nodded.

"Wow. So many of them."

"Yes. This is a common area in Lisbon for hot air balloons," Gus explained.

"I see." I answered.

Gus began the process of switching the gas off slowly as the balloon floated in over the beautiful patchwork landscape. Elliot wrapped his defined arms around me, nibbling on my ear. I giggled like a little schoolgirl. "You're tickling me. *Stop it.*"

I reached in my purse, discreetly picking up the infrared dust. Gus was preoccupied working on bringing the balloon down to a smooth landing. I flattened the microfine powder along my fingertips so it wouldn't clump up on Elliot's back. I placed my hands on the bare skin of his back, caressing several times, rubbing it in. Kinda awkward, but he leaned forward with his spicy scent, making it easier to reach. I could feel his hard on rising. I smiled to myself.

"Am I, Ms. Clemens? I hope to do more than just tickle you later on. You're trying to seduce me right now, and that is a nasty game you're playing," Elliot warned playfully.

"I don't think we're going to be taking it that far anymore." I tightened up slightly.

"You can relax. It's a wish, an option for you if you so choose. We have already crossed that bridge though. Not like we can go back. Why would you want to?" Elliot charmed as the balloon lowered to the ground. The green fields gave the illusion of looking as if they were running towards us.

"I know what we've done. I have no regrets. One of those lucky nights," I said.

"Touché. I can't disagree with you on that one." The hot air balloon landed with a graze along the top of the grass, the bliss wearing off a little as my phone beeped. I opened the zipper on my purse and pulled out my phone.

Gus was busy conversing with Elliot *"So when we land..."*

I seized the moment. Hawk.

Really? I'm tracking him, you're aware. I assume you have an explanation for being there.

I closed my eyes as the angst of the precarious situation I was in sat heavy in my chest.

Darkness or light. Which side Sara?

16

HAWK

♟

The taste of what you can't have, that place where you cross the divide to selling your soul. Sara was knee deep in it. I'd warned her that she would face this. I warned her that Elliot was this type of man. That she was playing with fire. She was making it hard for me to nail this sucker.

When I tried to call her phone and share a message with her about the Viper, she didn't answer. A flash forced its way into my mind. *A balloon*. I'd crushed the thought, gone out for breakfast, came back and the thought was still there. A hawk circling. I'd abruptly strode straight to my computer; a nagging voice said it would have the answer. Sure enough, as soon as I logged into the mainframe two red dots hovered over the middle of Coruche. One cell number from Elliot, the other seemed familiar, making me frown. I traced it. *Sara*. I sighed deeply. I knew that obsessive feeling she was having. Problem was, Elliot was at the center of it all. The guy stole *my* girl right out from under me. Now my protege was fucking him. She didn't want to come right out and say it, but when I played the security tape back it showed Elliot at her villa and him not leaving until after the midnight hour. His white shirt was thrown on, buttoned up in the wrong holes. What it looked like, was exactly what it was. Sara had been fucked within an inch of her life.

I called her phone, huffing, as the frustration boiled over inside. I clicked off the phone.

My phone lit up. Private number. "Hawk here," I barked.

"Hey, hey – you alright? it's Dermas."

"Yeah, I'm good," I sighed with resignation. I pushed my jet-black hair out of my face, unclenching my jaw.

"You're early with the call. I thought our check in was later on today?"

"Yes. Good pickup. Got a security breach, so I'm about to head into a meeting. What you got for me?" he asked. His voice sounded panicked, which made the hair go up on the back of my neck. Not his usual behavior. Dermas was normally really calm.

"Secure line?" I asked him.

"Of course. Go ahead," he said simply.

"I have four names for you. Fabio Coron Vazquez, Juan Galvez, Miguel Herrera, Donte Guzman. I don't know if any others are involved right now. I have to work on a tap to get to them. Any ideas?"

"Ah... let me get back to you. I might have a source that can do that work."

"Okay, don't wait too late. They have already had two meetings, so something's about to go down. We need to get to them fast."

"No problem. Ms. Clemens? She enjoying her holiday?"

"As far as I know. She's good." A feeling told me *not* to tell Dermas what happened. I couldn't put my finger on it. His tone had changed in pitch when he asked about her. The same way mine did when I asked about Evana.

"Okay, just she asked me to run some prints on her

window for that creton Elliot allegedly sent after her. We're still trying to get a search warrant to Elliot's home. It's proving to be difficult."

"Huh. The man is a billionaire; he and his family have deep global pockets."

"Absolutely. I'm going to keep working on it. We'll catch the guy."

"Okay. Check back in a day or so, and meanwhile see if you can get me a wiretap device and I can work from there."

"Okay. Good work on the Istanbul case. It stalled the shipment to their Russian affiliates We have more time up our sleeve right now."

"Ok, good."

"Later, Hawk."

"Bye, Dermas."

His concern for Ms. Clemens sent a red flag up for me; shouldn't have. I gave her the number. I'd trusted the guy. I'd worked with him on and off on assignments for years. I stood quietly for a moment, turning to the eastern window in my light-filled villa just outside Almada. I dropped to the floor cross-legged, inhaling deeply, letting the stream of air fill my lungs. In and out until a trance-like feeling rested in my chest. The hawk appeared, it sat on a crumbling timber and weathered fence post, letting out a hawk call. It spread its valiant copper-toned wings. Blades of sweetgrass bent in the wind of open fields. Lilac clouds filled the sky overhead, joining suddenly behind the hawk, forming a column. I watched a rapid formation of air sweep across the length of the field. It decimated a whole grid of the golden field, taking everything in its wake. The hawk remained still, it's penetrating beady eyes looking at me, never wavering even though the tornado was inches from it. The word formed: 'informant' the Hawk cried again. 'Informant' and again.

'Informant.' I bowed my head to the hawk in prayer as the tornado stopped. I opened my eyes thankful for the clarity. I had every right not to trust Dermas. *He was an informant.* Now I just had to prove it. That's why Dermas was so accommodating and happy to visit Sara all the way from Washington before he left. He wasn't in the area at fucking all. She was surrounded by snakes and not those with snake medicine. They still didn't know about me, nor would they.

I was like a thief in the night – I would be the last thing they saw coming. I smiled. Secret weapons are always handy to have. This information I couldn't hold. I had to get to Sara asap.

I rose from my feet, looking at the clock; an hour had passed. Almost midday. I looked at the tracking device on the computer. They'd separated. Elliot was in a Lisbon location: Amadora. Sara was back in the vicinity; I'd already sent her a text message.

This time I rang her phone. "Done cavorting with the enemy?" I asked lightly.

"Don't start, Hawk," she warned.

"What do you know?" I reasoned.

She let out a pained groan. "My methods are a little mad, but they work. You wanted the tap. You have one."

"You know you did that last time and he found it." I kept on her case as I placed my hands behind my neck.

"I used the other one you gave me. The dust stuff, I put it on my finger and his back. Only holds for 48 hours, right?"

"Hmmm... nice work. It does, depending on how many times he showers."

"Okay. Wasn't easy."

"Alright now that you're done mixing business with pleasure, are you free or are you expecting a visit?"

"No visits. He knows not to come here. He had to go anyway... an emergency. You should be able to see."

"Okay, hold tight for a few hours. I need to give you the heads up on a few things. Watch your step."

"You sound scary right now. Do I need to be worried?"

I winced a little. "A little. Nothing I can't handle once we have enough evidence."

"I know what that means. I'll be waiting. Don't get busted."

"No chance of that, Mama. Looks like you might just be femme fatale of the year."

Sara giggled. "What can I say, I play to win. It's a lot of fun."

"Careful. Remember who you're dealing with."

"I do. Trust me."

"Okay. Let me get to work." From the green private investigator I first met, Sara had come a long way. A very long way. The dust might not hold that long. Same process I applied in Istanbul. I shook my head as the corners of my lips curled up with a chuckle. I logged into the system I created. The infrared dust would show the person it belonged to. The heat would assist in activating their voice through the thermal sensors in the powder. Sure enough, transmission was clear as a bell.

"Hey, Clope. What's news?"

"The feds are still on my ass. They have another clue. I don't know... I might need to disappear, boss. It's feeling like a little too much heat right now. I can't prepare the port like I want. I don't want any rats out in the yard. The feds are snooping around there."

"Money talks. Shut them up and make them go away. Clear it. The shipment is going to be operational in the next 28 days. Is that about that fucking rope you brought?"

"They don't have anything. What can they do with the rope? A lot of people have the same rope I brought."

"Shhh. You're talking from the burner, right?"

"Yeah, it's roasted after the call. I know the procedure, boss."

"Good. I gotta go. I have a meeting with the crew here."

"Alright, boss. Property sales are up from last night. Come through?"

"Yep. I saw it. Nicely done. Keep it up. We need that cover to stay legit."

"I hear ya. We got a $90 million property that just crossed the desk. We should be able to pull some strings and sell it. Tech guy wants to buy it."

"Okay, send me the details of that one. I wanna know more and what part of tech he works in."

At that point the thermal started making Elliot's voice drop in and out. I took off my headphones. This son of bitch thought he could rule the world, and by all accounts it looked like he was doing just that. I rose from my seat. Pity I wasn't here under different conditions. I paused as the sun sprinkled through my villa. I knew the next pit stop I had to make, at least I got the case update right from the horse's mouth.

I showered quickly, jumped in the car rental flying over to Sara's villa. I loved the new car scent smell of rental vehicles. Just like this one. The whole interior smelled of Armor All. Made me feel like a vagabond with all the travelling I did. To me and in my heart, I was a citizen of the world. If I was in the United States for three months of the year then it was just sheer luck. My heart tugged a little as a hotbed of guilt set in. I hadn't spoken to Evana. Her ethereal sweet face dropped in my mind, making me tingle all over. I couldn't wait to have her in my arms after all this. I knew she was busy and understood the ramifications of my job now. Still she was a woman. *My woman.* When I saw the frown on her face and her luminous wide eyes get sad as I told her about the latest case. I knew. She'd just dealt with the death of her father. The fallout. She'd loved Elliot even if she told me she was with him for convenience and lifestyle.

Sara was falling down a rabbit hole, and this was one I couldn't save her from. As I pulled off to the side of Sara's villa, I thought about how Evana would react when I told her

Sara was sleeping with someone who was technically her husband on paper.

I breathed in deeply, the memory of the tornado storm behind the hawk in my vision. It was Sara's. As I gripped the leather steering wheel, I pulled in and rode slightly uphill to Sara's white villa. I pulled my hands off the wheel and knocked. She answered, looked like she'd just gotten out of the shower herself. Her hair was wet; she was dressed casually and towel drying it.

"Well, don't stand there – come on in," she said, gesturing.

"Hey," I said as I moved past her to the light-filled apartment. She had a bunch of documents laid out in front of her.

"What's all this?" I pointed.

"I'm checking into the Portugal documents for extradition. I'm trying to see what we can do to get him back to the United States. You got here quick, you must have something to tell me."

I shrugged out of my jacket and rolled up my sleeves. I sat down at the table with her. Her private investigator face was back on. Looked like she'd returned to her senses.

"Can I get you a drink first? We got a lot to talk about. I can feel it. You have some things to tell me." The sunlight shone on the side of Sara's face, making her look golden. I smiled at her warmly.

"I have a lot to say and I have a lot to tell you," I sighed.

Sara brought two small glasses to the table along with a high-quality bottle of gin, tonic water and lime.

"Got to keep the calorie count low, you know. This is my go-to summer drink. Technically I'm still on holiday, so don't look at me like that."

I just gave her a head nod. "I'll take it. Let's talk about a few things, get a few things out of the way, first." Her face was blank as she waited for the penny to drop.

"I have the tape. I don't know if Piedre has a copy for insurance. Let's start with that." Sara licked the lime off her fingers, putting the clear liquid to her lips and sipping. Her big innocent eyes smiled at me over the glass.

"Okay, go ahead."

"First, purely based on timing, Elliot was in your room for far too long for it to be a chat situation." I watched her body language change as she shifted in the seat, staring behind me.

"Are you going to say it, or am I?" I asked.

"Shit situation, I know. I didn't plan on it. I didn't even know he was coming to my villa. What could I do?" She shrugged, lowering her eyes.

"Horseshit, Sara. You could have kicked him out. You're in a hell of a position right now. If they nail Clope, he might not talk but he's going to be a prime witness in the case. You're going to be high on the list for people they want to talk to. You know, that right? Colluding with the man who ordered the hit."

"No, because I'm undercover. How can they prove anything?" I stared at her long and hard, picking up my drink and sipping.

"Let's talk morals. What the fuck are you doing? He tried to kill Evana and you helped her get away. He sent a fucking assassin after her. What do you want me to say to Evana?" I said, more frustrated than I wanted to be.

Sara begged with her eyes and grabbed my sinewy forearm. "Please don't tell her. Let's just leave it. I don't know. If Elliot wasn't a criminal... I don't know, Hawk. He's not the person you think he is." Sara's long lashes lowered as I watched a tear splash into her gin.

"Sara, I don't know what the hell is going on with you, but there's plenty of single men who would date you. I know you're into a little danger, but this ain't the way to get your thrills. This guy does not give a shit about you. He's not going to care about you in the end. The man is ruthless. You won't get sympathy votes here," I spat out. "The man is twisted. He killed my girl's father then married her. The guy is a sick, twisted fuck."

She downed the drink and poured another gin, adding in some soda and then the lime. "It was one-time, Hawk. There's no way in hell you're giving me a lecture on treating women right. You need to shut up right now." She cut her eyes at me like glass.

"All of them were single. Let's start there... but come to think of it, I have fucked a couple of killers myself." I slammed my glass down. "That's not the same. I know how to detach. I'm an assassin."

Sara arched her eyebrow. "Well, maybe I could be one. Plus, I got you what you needed. Keep talking."

I scrunched my nose at her. "You've changed. I don't know you anymore."

"Enough." Her face spelled annoyance.

"Okay, here's the deal. FYI, the Viper came from the abandoned field behind the villa. Easy access – a back fence off in the west quarter of the hotel. Climbed on the roof and waited for the right time.

"Shit. I don't want to talk about that right now. It's too much to deal with." I watched as Sara's eyes went to glass.

"Hey, I'm sorry I wasn't here. I wanted to get here faster." I lowered my voice as I placed my hand on her arm.

"No. You can't always save me. I'm good now." She leaned her head back as she shuffled the papers on the desk.

"I know you're not okay, but we don't have to talk about it now. Have you spoken to Dermas at all since you've been here?"

"Yes. Why?"

"When did he call you?"

"Hmm... about ten minutes or so ago," she said slowly as her eyes shifted. "Hawk, what? What aren't you telling me?"

"What did he ask you about?"

"He asked if my holiday was going well and what I'd been up to..."

"And you told him what?"

"Nothing. I didn't mention the Viper. I just said that it was eventful."

"Why didn't you tell him about Elliot? Why didn't you tell him about the Viper?"

Sara spun her drink around on the table. "I don't know exactly... I got this funny feeling when he came to see me... I couldn't put my finger on it. I don't know... Just why would someone so high in ranks at US Homeland Security would drive all the way to New Jersey to see me? Surely he had better things to do with his time."

I smiled. "Okay we're on the same page. Good. He's an informant. In my meditation I saw him as an informant. Who to, I don't know, but that's the problem..." I trailed off.

"I know who," Sara responded in a chilly tone. "Elliot mentioned something to me." She paused momentarily. "He mentioned that he knew I was already coming here. I can't be certain, but maybe Dermas had been keeping an eye on me the whole time, like a minder."

"Yup. *That's it.* I need to get up. This is a real nice villa, by the way. Shame you only have a week to go." I looked out at the view of the Tagus River. The villa happened to be high enough to see out over it.

Sara put her head in her hands. "So much for blowing off steam."

"I could make a bad joke right now."

"Please don't," Sara lamented.

"Alright, I won't. I miss my lady."

"I never thought I would hear the day you said that."

I pftted at her. "You and me both. But hey – the day is here, and I'm so glad I came to my senses."

"Ugh. Soppy. Sit down and tell me the rest."

"What? As opposed to killers? That's your preference?" I

bit back. Sara rolled her eyes at me. "Alright, so Elliot has a date for a shipment in 28 days. It looks to be a pretty sophisticated arrangement. Kudos to getting that dust on him because it was valuable. If we can apprehend the shipment at Port Authority in New York, then we will hand it over to Homeland."

"So, we can haul in the bust, right? But it's still going to be hard to pin Elliot."

I placed my hands behind my head and stretched. "Miguel will be our link. I can taste it. He doesn't like Elliot. He thought he was going to smuggle his own guns on the boats through Port Authority without Elliot knowing. Now knowing your man..."

"He's not my man." She death stared at me as she sipped her water. I was grateful she wasn't on her third gin.

"Sure as hell could have fooled me. But hey, what do I know."

"Keep going." She had her game face on. Maybe the gin helped.

"If Elliot found out, there would have to have been a lover's tiff. He's the chink. I need to find out where he hangs out. If I can get to him, I can make him talk. Offer a bribe... an incentive to rat on Elliot. To call him out to Portugal authorities."

"I think that's a helluva an idea. It just might work."

I rocked back on my chair a little and spread my arms out wide. "I'm not bad, huh?"

"Except who the hell do you trust in Homeland now?" Sara added.

"I have sources. Let me clear them. Shit's getting twisted, and I need to know what kind of kickback Dermas is getting. It must be substantial... He works for the fucking government. Some men are just greedy douche bags."

"Power hungry is more like it."

17

SARA

♟

My head was back in the game... well, halfway. I was sitting smack bang in the middle of Lisbon reading extradition documents. The café I sat in reminded me of the interior of my New Jersey favorite. Low level black industrial lights filled with soft warm ambient light. Black chalkboards with cursive writing and menu items scrawled on them. The inside of the café was made up of exposed red brick. Two cool baristas with extraordinary coffee making abilities stood behind the machine, one with a red beanie sloped off his messy bedhead hair and rusty yellow jeans which looked like they were painted onto his legs. He boiled the milk as he chatted with the other barista with a punk style haircut wearing funky coveralls and an upper lip piercing. The coffee in Portugal was different, which I appreciated. Richer somehow, more authentic. The people and their cultures were different, too.

I thought of the women as being liberated and socially conscious as I watched two of them speaking with passion at the front window. They were facing the cobblestone streets of Lisbon where they'd just parked their vintage lady bikes. The men were prettier, brilliantly sharp dressers with a hint of rebelliousness. Light corduroy jackets, collar shirts with big loud colorful themes on them. *And the shoes!* Made me swoon. I needed another suitcase for the purchases I wanted to make. I guess that's where the similarities ended. Jersey mornings, people were always in a rush. I thought back to the mornings before 9 a.m. that I'd accidentally gone in there.

"Excuse me. I gotta be at work in five. Mind if I go before you?"

In and out. Some villagey color on the weekends but not as much as Portugal.

"Bom Dia" is a phrase I was hearing often. I learned this was 'Good morning' in Portuguese. A man who looked to be of Arab descent hugged another who looked like me. Other women of all shades greeted him with hugs and flowery kisses and an air of flamboyance. I smiled as I looked on with curiosity around me. Something I wished I could take back home to Jersey with me was the connected energy, fewer inhibitions. I looked down at my printed papers, sighing deeply. My mind drifted to Michael Sawyer's father, my long-standing client.

"Whatever it takes. Take down his empire, Sara. Keep making it hard for him. My son deserves justice. He didn't deserve to die like that." All I wanted was a little peace. Not to feel guilty. Why did I take on a billionaire? Why would I do that to myself? My stomach twisted up at the thought of it all. My decisions were coming back to haunt me. My dark hair hung over my shoulder as I poured over the documents, scanning for an opportunity to nail Elliot.

"Article II, crimes committed at sea...hmmm," I whispered out loud to myself.

My mind pieced it together, smuggling drugs across international waters would definitely hold up. To pin him would be another story. Miguel Herrera was the missing link.

What did I know about Miguel? From his photos he looked like a serious man. His eyes were dark and kind-of hard to read. Late forties, a small stocky build and, according to the records from Hawk, never convicted of any crimes. Didn't mean he never committed any. As I looked over the documents, I noticed something I'd missed. I'd run a report from my own sources. I had the full records of Lisbon police officials. I ran my finger down the list. The print out included photos. I hovered over a name as I matched up the faces. A Portuguese detective, a woman with dark brown hair and penetrating eyes. Ana Herrera. A lot of Herreras in Portugal. I sat back in my chair. I wondered if there was a connection. I looked back and forth at their pictures. Same nose. Same large foreheads. Same weird ass smiles. I pulled my phone out and took a picture of both of them sending it off to Hawk.

Are they related?

Let me know

Ten seconds later a phone call came in as the breakfast I ordered came out.

"Hey, that was quick."

"Yep. Sucks I can't come and meet you out in the open."

"Just wear a disguise."

"Elliot is on your ass. Trust me. He knows you have someone else you're talking to. I'm not going to risk it. You're right. That's his sister. She's on the force. Better yet, his cousin works for the Port of Leixões he's connected to the owner."

"Makes sense. How are you going to get to Miguel?"

"I'm going to find out where he hangs out and have a conversation with him. Plant a few seeds, you know what I mean?"

"Nice."

"Stay out of trouble."

"I'm not the one. Trouble seems to find me. Have you figured out what to do about Dermas yet?"

"I know for certain that Cooper, who is his superior, is clean." Hawk said.

"Okay, let's see how this pans out."

I watched my surroundings as people flowed in and out. A man with leathery olive skin and a saggy neck walked in and for some reason the hairs on the back of my neck stood up. I cast my eyes down to his shoes. Leather loafers, a tan beret, rust colored pants and a darkness that made the café feel heavy. As I worked my way up his body his beady dark eyes made contact with mine, latching on like a vice. I looked away first. I feared if I looked any longer I might fall into a pit of deep hell. I still had the phone clamped to my ear. I grabbed the water to soothe my now bone-dry throat.

"What happened, Sara. You went quiet. Who is it?" Hawk's senses were incredible.

"How about we talk about the festival a little later." I smiled into the phone. I knew Hawk had the tracker on. He would find out who it was. The beady-eyed man had his eyes still on me. I ignored him as his eyes drifted to the documents on the table. I quickly pulled them together and slid them into my handbag. He wasn't going away.

"Hello. How are you?" he asked in a buttery Spanish accent.

I tilted my head sideways slightly. "Fine thank you." I planned to drink my coffee and flee.

A hand laid flat on the table with a few large brass rings on it. The smile from the man was leery and I wanted to vomit.

"Why are you leaving so quickly? My name's Fabio. You might not know me, but I know you."

My eyes started to blink rapidly as all I saw behind them was white. My heartbeat sped up to a sickening pace. People in the café dispersed around him. Fabio was one of the four. I picked up my water and it took all elements of my mental control to keep my fingers steady on the glass. I brought it to my lips and drank.

I looked him straight in the eye. "I don't know how the hell you think you know me, but I can assure you I don't know you."

A smile swept across the man's face, revealing a gold-capped tooth. "Sure, you do. I'm the reason you're still alive. We should talk. You look very nice, sexy. Maybe there's something you can do for me," he said in the slimiest tone possible. The stench of his breath was staining my left ear. I jerked my head away from him. I was figuring out if he was within elbowing in the stomach distance. I held my poker face and calm disposition as Hawk walked in, I recognized him purely by height.

"Bom Dia meu Amor!" He was wearing a silk Versace shirt, black jeans and sunglasses. His hair was black, long and slicked back in an oily ponytail. My eyes bugged out as he approached me with his muscular arms. Fabio narrowed his dark dangerous eyes with suspicion. He lifted his arms, recoiling in confusion. "Who the hell are you?" he griped.

"I'm the boyfriend. Pleased to make your acquaintance." My body heaved with an internal laugh. I went from being wrapped in a blanket of terror to wanting to burst into a welcome respite of laughter. Hawk held out his huge sinewy hand to Fabio. Fabio's lip curled into a dirty snarl as he ignored it and tapped on the wooden table with his hairy knuckles. "I'll be seeing you," he sent a warning shot. He tried to sidestep Hawk, who grazed his upper bicep. Hawk held his sunglasses down, staring at Fabio dramatically.

Hawk whispered a sentence as people moved around us, curious at the scene being played out. "Move seats. I need to face the door," he said.

"Okay." I quickly swapped seats as Hawk sat down on the other side.

"Those pants are interesting." I arched my eyebrow at him, he flashed me a wide grin.

"You like? A little Portuguese flavor. Something I threw together at the thrift shop."

"Coming to the rescue once again. Thank you."

"I caught him on the infrared. What the hell was that about?" Hawk asked.

"I don't exactly know. He said he knows me. He's one of the four. Fabio."

Hawk's face held a look of knowing. "Elliot."

"Elliot?"

"Yeah, I haven't shown you the tapes. Elliot called someone to come help him with the cleanup. Wanna take a guess of who it was?"

Shocked, I registered the news. "Fabio and his crew? This just gets more twisted. I can't believe it."

"Right. So now you have a situation. I'm thinking if Elliot knew he wouldn't be so happy that his main side chick was getting hit on," Hawk teased as he scratched his scalp.

"I hope that wig itches the shit out of you."

Hawk waggled his finger at me. "Temper, temper little lady."

"You are a thorn in my side. You really are."

"One that you want there, otherwise Fabio might have gotten his way."

I jutted my jaw out at him. "Not a chance in hell. I got my Glock locked and loaded in my purse. I would have no problem shooting him in his lady killer parts."

"Ouch." Hawk placed his hands under the table, covering his balls.

"So, if he knows about you do you think he will stay away?"

"Not necessarily. I think you should check out where you're staying – that's for sure."

"How many days are you here for?" Hawk enquired.

"I have five days to go. This shit is crazy. I mean, what the hell do I do about Dermas?"

"I'm working on him. I have an insider trying to trace his records to see how long he's been sold out."

I tossed a hand through my hair as the mess continued to unfold. Trouble was, I didn't know how deep it ran.

"Chill out. It's time to use this situation to your advantage. Send Elliot a text letting him know Fabio hit on you. Meanwhile, let's get you moved out of the villa now."

"Time to play." My adrenaline was peaked at an all-time high. I sent off a text to Elliot.

I just got a visit from a friend of yours. Ten minutes later a reply came back.

Oh yeah who?

Fabio. Made a pass at me

Can't say I blame him. I will take care of it Who is the man with the greasy ponytail?

I slowly rolled my head around the café.

"And?" Hawk asked impatiently.

"Elliot is here, or he's got someone undercover watching me. He just asked about your greasy ponytail." I said slowly, barely moving my lips. I watched as the sounds of the café filled my ears. The girls sitting at the front window had left, they were now replaced with two twenty somethings on their laptops, cross legged, sipping their coffees, pointing to their screens. One older gentleman with sprinklings of a salt and pepper beard was with an older white-haired lady eating sweets. A relatively normal café scene. Hawk's sunglasses were on as he sat silent.

"Behind me. Don't look too hard, there's a gentleman on a laptop. Notice how the laptop is faced towards you?"

I picked up my cup which had the last dregs of my coffee in it. "Yes. I can see him. Thirties I would say, dark navy jacket and blue jeans. Curly black hair?"

Hawk smiled and poured water into the glass in front of

him. "That's the guy. Look at the camera on the back. He has it facing you. He's recording right now. I wanna bet that if I go over there he will quickly scramble and shut the computer down." Hawk dipped his head to the side. "Move to the outside. You've paid already, yes?"

My head was facing out to the street as I spoke quietly to Hawk. We were a good one- two combo. "Yes, all covered. I see. I'll meet you across the street. I'll see if I can ID him with a photo. Work it." I gave him a wicked smile as I slid from around the seat and moved outside. Hawk with his huge presence walked over in his ridiculous pirate get-up to the guy in the corner.

I was already outside, moving through the small crowd. I turned to watch the show. As predicted the man scrambled to pack up his computer as soon as Hawk came over. I watched as Hawk discreetly placed a small dot on the back of the laptop. The man crab legged away from Hawk with intense fear in his eyes. Even his curls started shaking as he scooted out the door with his backpack. I whipped my phone out in my hand as he struggled with the bike at the front of the shop. I fired off a round of shots in quick succession. My iPhone clicked with every shot.

Hawk emerged from the café as I heard cars honking their horns in the busy Portugal square.

"You get them?"

"Yep." I giggled a little as the wig had shifted slightly, and now was lopsided on Hawk's head.

"You have a hair problem."

"I realize. Don't look now, but at 3'oclock we got Fabio and his boys heading into the café. C'mon, let's go. There's a taxi rank around the corner."

We sped up into a light jog as we blended and weaved between the people. Hawk snatched off his wig and ruffled his thick dark hair.

"What do you think? Could you take me home to mother?"

"You'll pass, minus the shirt." Hawk grinned as he unbuttoned the Versace shirt and threw it in the trash, revealing a white wife beater. He whistled at the white Portuguese taxi as we both jumped in.

18

SARA

♟

A scruffy younger guy wearing a hat opened his taxi to us. "Olá. Where to ladies and gent?"

"Almada, as fast as you can," Hawk directed.

The man gripping the wheel beeped at a young lady on a teal vintage bike with a basket full of bread. She reminded me of a scene straight out of Paris. The scruffy man grinned as I looked closer; I realized he had a goatee. "You got somewhere to be, boss?" he asked Hawk, who was silently checking items in his backpack. My head was crystal clear.

He handed me a small button-like device. "Detonator. Just in case."

"Hawk-"

He gave me a deathly stare as the driver compiled, putting his foot to the metal while ducking in and out of the helter skelter Portugal traffic. I witnessed him leaning forward, beeping at people along the way. He was enjoying the thrill of the chase. Meanwhile, I was knocking around to and for in the backseat.

"Okay," I said mildly.

We made it back to Almada in quick time. Hawk pointed through the middle of the vehicle. "See the villa at the back there? That's the one." I had that nasty situation where my palms were starting to feel clammy. The pressure was on. Maybe Fabio and his crew had already left the café.

"No problemo. That was fun for me. I think in my next life I would like to be a rally car driver," the enthused driver said.

Hawk laughed. "You did good, my friend. Glad you could get us here in one piece."

The driver signaled the ok symbol with his hand. "Of course. I'm one of the best drivers in the city." The taxi settled to a stop.

"How much?" Hawk asked.

"Nineteen Euro." The driver whistled to himself as Hawk pulled the money from his pocket and handed it over.

"Thanks, keep the change."

"Thank you, fellow citizens. Have a wonderful day," he sang out cheerfully.

I got out of the car fuming.

"How did Elliot think he could trust Fabio? They must have done business before together." I was angry at him. Angry at myself. Angry at the seductive imp living inside of me and the fact that it was greedy and wanted more of Elliot. The deep part of me that was excited about the whole escapade and living for the thrills.

My phone rang before Hawk could answer me. I threw him my villa keys so I could answer the phone as we walked towards the oak door.

"I knew you weren't doing this all alone. You're safe – Fabio is off your case. I won't let anything happen to you. Nice little tactic there in the café," he crooned.

"I should have known you would call. What tactic? I was enjoying a coffee with a friend and your sleazebag associate came in."

"I'm sorry. He didn't know you were off limits. He surely

does now." I mouthed to Hawk. *Elliot.* I looked around my villa twice and stepped inside.

Elliot kept talking. "That won't stop me, you know. So, who is the guy? Do I need to be worried about him?"

I breathed in the exhilaration of flirting with danger. "Why? Are you jealous?"

"Careful, Sara. Like I've always said, I'm a man who gets what he wants. I always have been. You don't want me to fly into a jealous rage. Remember what happened with Evana." Elliot's rich husky tone held a hint of danger. Hawk gave the all clear signal as he cased the rooms. I heard Elliot sigh. "Work with me, Sara. I want to show you more of Portugal. I'm sorry I got called away from the meeting. I had a whole day planned for us, not to mention the place I'd planned to take you that night." Elliot spoke erotically into the phone.

My body was starting to flush with tempestuous desire; my panties were getting wet. A hot vision flashed in my mind of Elliot stroking between my folds, his masculine hips rocking me into ecstasy with his lengthy cock. My throat caught fire as I smothered back a desperate whimper.

"Elliot."

"Uh-huh. I heard that. I got what you need. Stop denying what's going on here. Come and get it. I'm coming to get you tonight whether you like it or not." I had no time to answer. I clicked off the phone. Hawk was in the other room checking for bugs and devices. I listened as his footsteps came into the large space minutes later. I stooped down to the fridge and grabbed two beers. I listened for the pshhh as I released the lid. I needed to cool down after that conversation. The visions of us in the bedroom were coming back strong and fast. I felt my body reacting as if Elliot had an invisible string to my coochie. I needed to see him again.

It's not that big a deal. You're still working the case while you're working him. It's good for you. Not hurting anybody. Do it. Go to his villa tonight. Do him.

I blinked my eyes rapidly as if trying to erase the memory of the call. Hawk picked up the beer on the marble counter-top. "You're sweating. What did he say?"

"Ah. He's called off Fabio. I think I'm fine here, Hawk. I can handle him. I got what you needed for the case. I can see if he has any intel lying around. I know what I'm doing."

Hawk chugged down his beer. "You sure you do? 'Cause I don't think you have anything under control. I told you what this man does. Seducing women is his forte. You better decide right now what side you're playing on, because when duty calls – and it will, you're going to have to make a decision." Hawk's dark eyes penetrated my soul and I knew I couldn't hide from him. I turned my face to the blinding sunlight that was filtering onto the villa timber boards. I pulled the curtains together and drank more cold beer.

"It will be fine. You need to trust me more. I'm as committed to nailing him as you."

"And getting nailed." Hawk's sarcasm flew back at me with a resounding crunch. I gave him a smirky eye roll, but he sighed. "I don't want to sound like a buzz killer. You're a grown woman. Go in equipped at least. I need you to secure a new wire when you're in there. Question him. Start breaking him down. If you're going to play the role of femme fatale then this is the next level."

I cricked my neck and smiled. "Okay, tell me what we need to know…" I breathed hard, the pace of my heart quickening, causing a palpitation to flutter.

Now more than ever I was aware of Hawk's height. The full length of him stood up full scale to confront me. "Sara. You sure you know what you're doing?"

"Yes, I got it," I confirmed, my body was hot with the gross excitement building inside of me.

"Okay, we need that manifest. It's gotta be in his phone. I want you to sweep it." Hawk's hard-lined jaw clenched as as my eyes roamed his face in the light. Hawk opened his back-pack and pulled out a second button–like device.

"You're going to need a full minute to activate the scan. Stick this magnet over the top of it and it will download all the data in his phone. Be quick about it. It will automatically flow through to me. Think you can do it?"

"Yes, I got it, I told you," I responded with an irritated voice.

Hawk eyed me with amusement. "It's not going to be as easy as you think, but I'll give you the benefit of the doubt. I did underestimate you. You did better than expected."

I shook my head at him ignoring the jibe. "Listen, I'm staying, I'm not leaving. I came on holiday and I paid for this villa. I already survived the Viper. I'm not going to let this Fabio guy scare me, no matter who he sends. Back me up." The resoluteness was building up inside of me.

"I'm not far away. Take this, too. I will leave it right here on the bench." Hawk held up two small buttons in the light. "Both of them are highly charged bombs. They pack a punch. Two-minute timer on both. Courtesy of the British Intelligence Unit. Remember red. They are different to the magnets I gave you."

"Wow, what other gadgets have you got?"

"Wouldn't you like to know?"

"You're not going to be listening in on me, are you?" Hawk rolled his eyes and laughed so hard it shook the table.

"I could think of nothing worse. Plus, the infrared powder you put on Elliot has worn off. I won't be listening in. I gotta talk to my girl."

I felt the pang of guilt hit my stomach. "Evana?"

"Yes, I'm sick of this clown Elliot. The only good thing about the guy is he brought us all together." I didn't answer because quite frankly I didn't know how. Me confronting Evana and what I'd done was something I would need to address. I pushed it down, way down. My mind wouldn't let me confront the situation right now. The sun had dropped in the sky a little as the afternoon hit, casting dark shadows in the villa.

"I gotta go. I got a date with a hot blonde." Hawk tipped the end of my nose as I scrunched it away from him.

"Hey," I swiped at him. "Say hi to Evana for me," I said timidly, feeling the overwhelming guilt inside.

"Will do." Hawk, with his imposing figure, turned to me. "Be careful, Sara. Don't say I didn't warn you." I listened as he shut the oak villa door behind me.

As Hawk left, I held myself – placing my arms around my body, the feeling of vulnerability becoming very apparent, knowing Elliot was coming for me. I went to the cabinet to pour myself a drink. I wanted to have something in my hands. Something to hold onto... anything.

Could I really do this?

Could I really continue to fool myself?

To have the belief that I didn't have feelings for this man?

This relationship was like tripwire, if I fell off I would get fried.

I poured myself a drink as my hands, trembling, brought it to my lips. Erotic images penetrated my mind like a wicked kaleidoscope. Half an hour passed as my brown eyes watched the door. A thump on the roof made me hunch my shoulders in fright. The noise was followed by the beating wings of a bird, so I relaxed, blowing out a repressed breath.

I sipped the white wine, letting the giddiness take me over for a minute. The clock chimed as I watched the golden minute hand click over. I sat listening to the sound of my own breathing for the next ten minutes until I couldn't take it anymore. I went to the villa closet and pulled out my I-hope-to-get-lucky lingerie. A smile curved on my lips as I shuffled through my bag until I found my black silk bra and underwear set. I ran my fingers over it, twisting it back and forth in my fingers with a salacious smile.

I left my clothes behind on the ground and stepped into the hot shower. Lathering the luxurious creme body wash over my slender athletic frame, I let the raspberry and vanilla notes soothe me. I slipped on my seductress outfit under my white sundress, reveling in the role I was about to play. I strained my ears as a soft knock came at the door, listening in case I missed it. A twisted hitch in my throat. I was still feeling sexy from the wine. *No, I heard right.* My stomach fluttered as I placed my hand across it, trying to settle it down. I breathed out, letting the adrenaline run its course through my wired system.

I glided to the door and opened it to a sex machine on legs. Elliot's darkened eyes chased my charged body down. *"Sara."* The call of my name on Elliot's tongue floated through the air like a haunting flute note playing my favorite symphony. I gave him the same service. Head to toe he was every inch the man, pure electric heat radiating from him. His teeth pulled at his sexy bow-shaped lips as he smoothly wrapped his muscular arm around my waist, pulling me chest to chest with him. We were still in the middle of the door. In plain view. I became conscious of it and fisted a handful of Elliot's collared shirt, pulling him inside the door. I splayed my hand on his chest feeling over the hardness of his well-defined pecs. His hand dropped lower, cupping my ass. I watched as he closed his eyes, sniffing my neck. "You smell damn good. We might not make it to my villa." Elliot grabbed my thigh and moved me to the counter. I fumbled my fingers behind me for the detonators Hawk gave me. I distracted Elliot with a sultry moan. He fell for it.

"Elliot," I breathed.

"Uh-huh," he replied huskily as he let up from the fire kisses he left on my throat.

"Umm. I wanna see your villa. We should go," I coaxed as I discreetly slipped the tiny magnetic devices in my sundress pocket. I massaged my fingers into the base of Elliot's scalp as our tongues danced to the syncopated rhythm of intense lust. It turned me on to know that he was turned on. I had to steady myself against the counter from the furnace that raged between us. As we drew breath, I smoothed Elliot's hair over with a wicked smile.

"Okay, now we can go," he replied with a throaty chuckle. He interlocked his masculine fingers with mine quietly as my eyes darted around the villa to see if I forgot anything. He led me out as I locked the door behind me.

Remember what you have to do Sara. Scan his phone. Get the data.

I couldn't remember the walk over the threshold to Elliot's villa. I just saw his feet and mine in time, moving effortlessly. I don't know why he wouldn't be concerned with all the cameras functioning. The thumping in my chest let me know all of my senses were wildly alive. They were tingling with anticipation, tapped in like a live wire to Elliot. The violet plume of the sky brought in the darkness as we moved through the shadows.

We arrived at Elliot's villa, which was three times the size of mine. Arched walkways with three entries. Automated downlights drenched us in light as we approached. Elliot dropped my hand to open the honey oak doors. I ran my fingers over the walls briefly; they felt as if they'd been standing since ancient times. I watched closely, listening to the ragged rise and fall of my breath as he turned the key. Not a villa, a house. Opulent luxury surrounded us right down to the tablecloths. His villa was bathed in light, wide and open. Elliot flicked on the light, cream marble floors and a heavy knight's long sword hung on the left side of the wall. Elliot walked over to the round bar, pulling down two glasses.

"Drink, beautiful?"

"Yes." The overwhelming aura of the place itself, including the sheer sexiness of Elliot, wouldn't let me speak.

He handed me a glass of white wine, our fingers transferring electricity. I didn't want the wine – I wanted him. He watched me through the darkened lens of desire as I sipped the liquid courage. I swayed lightly from foot to foot with my glass in hand as Elliot closed the gap between us. His arm slid around to cup my ass as I licked the wine from his lips.

"Shall we dance?"

I giggled. "There's no music, though."

"Then I'll put some on," he countered softly. He gently clutched my hand leading me down a step into a sunken lounge room.

"Okay." My loss for words continued as I stepped with him. I looked at the spiral staircase right in front of us and knew that's where we were headed sooner rather than later. A large TV screen and a huge cream couch sat on the left along with a beautiful oak shaped table in the open plan area. He clapped his hands and spoke out loud.

"Play the rumba." His pearly whites grinned as the percussion beat dropped in around us, increasing the passion flaming under the surface between us. A sultry drumbeat with a Spanish flavor brought the room to life. Heat ran through my veins as Elliot's piercing ocean blue eyes centered on me.

"You dance the rumba?" I breathed in amazement as I placed my wine down on the coffee table.

"I do a lot of things, Ms. Clemens. I told you, you need to get to know me more." He held out his hand and I placed it in his. His hips were already gyrating and making me want to launch into his arms. I held steady, accepting his invitation. A symbol of trust... well, as far as you could trust a criminal you're sleeping with. In a swift moment and deft touch, he spun me in towards him, holding my elbow so I wouldn't fall.

I adjusted quickly as he held me tightly against his hard, muscular frame. He breathed in my scent and flung me out again, my hair releasing, flying around me as my sundress opened wide. My chest opened celebrating the madness of it all. I body rolled with a few moves of my own and came into him.

"Ms. Clemens, you are a lot more surprising than you let on. I knew there was a fire burning inside of you."

I laughed as Elliot grabbed my wrist. "My father is from the Islands, what do you expect? We know how to dance." I placed my hand on his shoulder as our hips moved in time with the music. I allowed the beat to take me away, understanding that Elliot and I had a soul connection that couldn't be explained. I felt the outline of his phone in his left pocket. I made a mental note to remember what he did with it once we got upstairs. If we made it... judging by the hard bulge in Elliot's pants rubbing against my leg, I knew it might be a task.

The beat of the music only amplified the palpable tension between us. Elliot's hands lingered, making their way to the outline of my breasts, skimming the length of me.

The phone Sara. Don't forget the phone.

My caramel eyes lingered on Elliot's face, the softness behind his icy blue waters shocked me. My brain led me back to shore quickly.

Remember he killed Evana's father, he ordered hits on innocent people. Remember Sara. My body and my heart were running two different stories.

Elliot briefly released me, stopping the music from playing. I brushed back my ebony locks as beads of sweat formed on my forehead. Silently he took my hand before I could catch my breath, leading me upstairs. I touched the magnets in my pocket, biting my lip from apprehension. *How the hell was I going to pull this off?* Maybe I wasn't cut out for it. No turning back now, the clock was ticking loudly in my head.

The winding staircase in itself was magnificent. Apparently, Elliot had a thing for them. Majestic paintings and sculptures were aligned in the corridor the whole way along. My toes sank into the plush carpet; it felt like quicksand. The bedroom door was open, it was like stepping into another house almost. A dim amber glow lit up the room as we entered, bathing the room in light. The beat of the music was still rumbling inside of me. I took the opportunity to take control of the moment as Elliot stopped in front of the queen size bed. Elliot's face was cast in a half glow as he spoke.

"Are you fully recovered now?" he asked.

"Yes, I am. I'm feeling pretty good right about now," I breathed in a sexy tone.

"Are we ready for round three?" I watched as Elliot's lips sung their song to me.

"Stop talking," I said. Elliot ran a hand through my hair as I purred. He quickly disposed of his shirt as I let my fingers walk down his chest and over the ripples of his abs that he'd no doubt carved with countless hours in the gym. I dropped my head, feathering kisses, bending to my knees. A low primal moan escaped from his lips. I was about to unlock the gates of hell inside of this man. A secret smile coming over my lips, I unzipped his jeans, taking his underwear down with them. Elliot's eyes were closed. I watched as his phone slid out of his pocket. I slid it under the left wing of the bed. My plan was in full effect.

His erection burst free as my lips curled around him. One of my hands supported the base as my other hand twitched in my pocket. My breath heightened. My pulse was omnipresent, beating solidly in both my chest and in my neck. I fumbled briefly, drawing Elliot back to the bed. He didn't flinch as I worked the tip of him. I managed to place the magnet on top of his phone. Out of my peripheral vision I saw a tiny green flash. It worked. My heart rate lowered for a moment. I refocused my energy back to the moment, letting the imp possess me. I listened to a man on the edge. "Stop! You're not going to do what you did last time, come up here." He lifted me to my feet and swung me onto the bed. With delicacy he lifted off my white dress, his pace more intense. My bra sprung free, releasing my caramel breasts as he hurriedly wrenched my underwear off. Elliot lifted my legs to his shoulders as I marveled at the intensity in his eyes. He ran a hand down the middle of body landing at my sweet entrance. He lightly placed his fingers in the folds, dragging my nectar to his mouth.

"Mmm... sweet." One touch and my body were on the verge of a sweet eruption. He watched my reaction as I writhed underneath him for more. He arched his brow at me. "See, that's what you do to me, Ms. Clemens." I watched as Elliot angled himself to enter, I breathed a sigh of relief as he rocked with the same rhythm as he danced. His hips moving in time with mine as I met him with pace, bucking against him. He set the tone this time, not letting me move any quicker, by gripping my wrists lightly on the silken sheets. My inner walls expanded and contracted as I heard the faint beep of his phone. *Shit.* He didn't react; his complete focus was on me, and servicing my body. He let out a grunt of satisfaction. I ran my fingers over his chest running them in circles. With every thrust, the veins in his neck surfaced, our bodies slickened with sweat from the intense passion we had for one another. Just as I felt my body tightening and for all of the light to go out, he kissed my foot and ran his hot tongue along my inner thigh, causing my eyes to widen in exquisite frustration.

"*Wait*... I'm going to get you there. No need to rush, Ms. Clemens." Elliot's husky lullaby returned. His silver tongue made its way to my promised land as my fingers caressed his scalp.

He wasted no time, finding my pleasure button as my body exploded like shattered glass. My mind went blank like a sheet of paper and my heart rate skyrocketed. Every inch of me tingled in sweet rapture. Elliot didn't stop there as he swiftly laid down beside me, turning me on my side as he entered behind me. His phone beeped again. This time I saw his head rise to get the phone. I grabbed him. "*No!* Finish what you started." My heartbeat rose, the next move life or death. Elliot didn't disappoint, his darkened devilish eyes wrapped his arms possessively around my breasts, cupping them. I could hear his ragged breaths as he entered with his thickened length from behind. I pressed my body back into him, this felt more heartfelt, intimate, as he nibbled at my ear. The friction increased as he quickened his strokes. I matched him while he kneaded my breasts softly as he prised my channel open by placing a knee in between for easier access.

"Sara." I waited for the explosive moment as the sweat flowed from my face and Elliot crashed, falling off the cliff into orgasmic bliss. I licked my lips in joy, our fragmented breaths causing us both to take a moment to recover.

"What are you doing to me?" he asked.

"I could ask you the same thing."

The afterglow of sex didn't derail me from what I had to do. "Baby, could you get me a glass of water?" I asked after a couple of minutes. Elliot kissed my forehead with tenderness.

"Sure. I'll be back," he said gently. I watched as his sexy form left the dimly lit room.

I leapt from the covers and slid his phone towards me. I took the small magnetized device from his phone and slipped it into my white dress. I frowned, it was as if Elliot didn't view me as a threat. That was a huge mistake on his part. I slipped back under the silken sheets, a drowsiness coming over me. He returned with two large glasses of water and placed them on the counter. An amused smile wrapped around my lips as I surveyed his delicious body from head to toe openly.

"Don't start what you can't finish, Ms. Clemens," he warned in response.

I giggled while taking the water, needing it. "I won't. I won't. Promise."

Elliot's Achilles' heel, his weakness for women was about to be his ultimate downfall, because I played to win.

19

ELLIOT

S he'd left at morning light. As soon as I watched her walk out the door I wanted her to run back through it. I looked at it, hoping, wishing, thinking she would just come back at any moment.

"I have to go now. I have to get ready to go home. I've had the time of my life with you, Elliot. It's definitely been an interesting ride." She'd paused for a beat as I felt at home in her warm, dark brown eyes. "If there's anything you want to tell me before I go back to the United States, you need to tell me now."

I'd given her a funny look as I slipped out of the bed. "What would that be? I don't have anything to say other than... *Stay*. That's what I want you to do. Stay with me. Be together with me."

She'd shaken her glossy ebony locks. "No. You know I can't do that. You're still wanted for questioning for the Michael Sawyer murder. That's why I'm asking you, Elliot."

She'd narrowed those pretty diabolical eyes at me. "If there is anything I can help you with now, then you should tell me. Anything at all. Let me know now." A plea. Letting me know she was in my corner.

I'd turned up my lips at the corners with a nonchalant shrug of my naked shoulders. I'd watched her pull the straps of her sundress up. She looked like an angel in white, but I knew she wasn't, because the devil comes in many forms.

"Again, there's nothing to know. I'm going to miss you, Ms. Clemens. You're always on my mind. I can't seem to get you out of it." I crossed the room, quickly scooping her up into a soul-crushing kiss. I wanted my imprint on her. I wanted her to feel the heat I held inside for her. She responded like I wanted. She trembled with desire as I released her. My specialty.

"I'll miss you, too," she'd said softly, running her delicate fingers along my jawbone.

"I'd better go. Good luck, Elliot." She'd blown me a kiss and walked out of my life. I'd been calm because I knew it wasn't the end for us. We would come back together. Somehow, someway.

As she left, I searched for my phone. I'd heard it beep a couple of times during the night. I knew it was business, but I'd wanted to concentrate on Sara. I pulled on my jeans and spotted it near the edge of the bed. Made sense. It must have fallen from my jean pocket. A message from Donte flashed on it.

Small test run. Let's say two days. Fabio sending through channels. Confirm?

Confirm – go ahead. Send details. I replied.

A text came back instantly. *Done. Shipment placed File no. 234709 check. 10pounds.*

Good.

I got to work and made a call. "Dusty, it's Robert," I heard the beeping of cranes in the background and the ship's horn blowing.

"Hey hey, boss – how you doin'?"

"Everything's peachy on my end. I've got something I need you to keep an eye on for me."

"Go ahead, boss. What you need?"

"Check shipment manifest 234709. Arriving in two days. 10 pounds. Cargo ship starting Port of Leixões, changeover at Mexico, check it, you'll see. Take care of it and stay on watch. Can you do that for me?"

"Consider it done."

"You got a nice little bonus coming your way as well for your trouble," I stated.

"Can't get better than that. Got a bigger shipment after that?"

"Yes, keep you posted on it," I confirmed.

"Okay, bye, boss. Keep 'em rolling in. We got you."

"You're looking good for a promotion, Dusty. Keep it up."

He chuckled. "I'm all ears. I got mouths to feed and a daughter to put through college."

"Exactly. I got you. I'm on the run. Keep me posted. Same procedure."

"'Kay. Alright, got a shipment. Talk to you later, boss."

"No problem." I clicked the phone dead. I swore Sara's scent wafted through my nose. Vanilla and musk. I did smell her. She'd left her scarf behind, a tangerine one. I brought it to my nose, inhaling her sweet perfume.

What was this feeling I was having? Sadness. An emotion that had long left my icy cold heart, but now I felt it thawing. And with Sara's departure, the acute pain hurt so good... So *this* is what it felt like to be in love. I drank my morning coffee, allowing the new feelings to wash over me. I wanted to be with Sara. *To love her*. Properly. I didn't know if that was even possible in our worlds.

I snapped back to the task at hand, sipping my coffee, letting the wake-up elixir do its job. I placed the brightly-colored scarf in my pocket with a smile as I raked one hand through my hair in frustration.

What the fuck was I going to do?

How was I going to make this shit work with Sara?

Did she even feel the same?

Everyone knew I was a ruthless tiger in the boardroom and on the streets of New York and L.A. Hell, globally. But this was different. This woman had opened up the light in my soul. She was a real hellcat, and there was every possibility I was getting played at my own chess game. But I didn't care. I needed the challenge.

I heard a knock at the door. I padded to open it barefoot with no top. I opened it to the sexy maid, who I now longer cared for. Judging by the sultry look she gave me she still cared for me.

"Ola, do you need anything cleaned, Mr. Elliot?" She looked up at me through her long lashes as I shot a weak smile at her. I lifted up my mug.

"If you could bring me some more coffee, that would be great. I've run out." I replied. I must admit, she was my taste. I normally would have hit that without blinking, but this strange phenomenon was happening to me where I only wanted Ms. Clemens in my bed. If I couldn't have her, though, I doubt it would last... A man is not a camel after all.

"You good now?"

"Yes, life is better. I'm so happy now. You changed my life."

"Then why are you still working here?" My eyebrows connected in a furrow.

Isabella collected the clothes I wanted dry cleaned from my couch. She flicked her hair back, staring into my eyes with a dopey grin.

"I came to say goodbye. I finish in two days. Piedre is not happy. He wants me to stay."

I finished the last of my coffee, I had to get in touch with Fabio to organize a few things.

"Too bad. Like I said, you're too pretty to be working here

and putting up with this shit." I grabbed her chin and gave her what she wanted. I kissed her supple lips, just a taste and stepped back, satisfied. She licked her lips, hungry for more, her eyes still closed for a moment longer. She opened them in shock, realizing I wasn't going to continue.

"Você é uma provocação,"she breathed in a steamy tone.

My brow knitted together trying to piece together what she said to me. "It sounded good, but what did you just say to me?"

She let out a light-hearted giggle. "I said, Mr. Elliot, that you are a tease. I would like to be with you one time, but you don't want me like the other men do."

I smiled at her as the sunlight beamed through the curtains. I put my mug down as my phone beeped. "Trust me you're wrong about that. Just that I think I'm-" I stared into space for a moment searching for the right words to say.

"You're what?" she said as she held up the blue dry-cleaning bag.

"I think I'm in love."

She laughed some more as she moved to the kitchen to clean up. "You don't know of amar?"

I frowned again, I supposed I should really learn Portuguese properly if I was going to be living here. "Amar means love," she explained as she wiped down the bench.

"No. Not until now. But I've done a lot of damage I'm not sure I can redeem myself," I lamented with a heavy sigh.

"You never know unless you tell her. She might feel the same way. You seem to be very kind. I like you."

"That's where you're wrong, li'l lady. I'm ruthless. You just don't know it." I cautioned.

She giggled again. "You're funny, Mr. Elliot, and very sexy. You saved my life from all these men who wanted to use me. You're my hero. Now I can live my life freely." Without warning she threw herself at me. Her soft breasts hitting my naked chest as I grabbed her around the waist. She planted a juicy kiss on my lips and I yielded. *Who was I to refuse her?* I pushed her back from me after a moment longer because the only lips I really wanted to taste was Ms. Clemens.

"Did you put some away in a bank account like I said?" I chastised.

"Yes," she said simply as she resumed making the silver sink sparkle.

"Well I have to get to work now, if you'll excuse me. I'm happy for you." I looked around the room, spotting a notepad in the corner with a pen. I wrote down a number on it. I handed it to her. "Here's my private line. Don't give it to anyone. If you need anything just call me." I smiled. Who knew if I might change my mind...

"Thank you, you're no devil. There's something sweet inside of you. You just don't show." Her soft brown eyes lingered on me for a moment. I shook my head, turning on my heel. Women were like putty in my hands, they could never see until it was too late for them.

I moved to the back of the villa, enjoying the morning sun hitting my face. One more call to make.

"Heyyy, Mr. Elliot. You got the call from Donte, right?" Fabio asked.

"Yeah I did. Underway?"

"As we speak." There was hesitation in his accented voice. "Look, I want to apologize again about your girl. I didn't know you claimed her like that," Fabio said.

"Well now you're aware, if you go near her again I will slit your throat myself."

"Now look-"

"No, you look. Don't test me on this, Fabio. She's not one of those," I warned.

"Alright, we talked about it already. I just wanted to keep the airwaves clear."

I clenched my muscular jaw. "We're clear, don't worry," I

let the anger dissipate. I didn't even want Sara's name coming off his lips. "Let's make this money."

"Agreed. See you at the meeting."

"Good." I opened the double villa doors that looked out on the Portuguese countryside – a completely different view to the balcony at the front of the villa which overlooked the city of Portugal. I stretched my arms out wide, rolling my neck. Things were underway and I, Robert Elliot, was still king of the castle. I leaned my lean arms over the balcony, sucking in the air. My phone vibrated, twice, three times. I pulled it out of my pocket.

Photos of a blonde, the back of her. A group of women, she looked to be on set somewhere. Then came the call.

"Aye boss, do you see what I see?" A raspy Boston-accented Clope answered the phone.

"Where is she?" Evana. My wayward wife - soon to be dead.

"Looks like Paris. Wanna take out another hit?"

My blood was starting to boil and the vengeance streak that my DNA coded was rearing its ugly head like I knew it would.

"No. Hold tight. Stakes are too high. Where you calling from?" I confirmed with caution.

"Burner phone, we good."

"Good. No, you got heat on you, which means so do I. We got shipments rolling. Let's wait. Keep tracking her. Find out who is protecting her. Someone has her covered. Any more evidence?"

Clope's killer laugh came through the phone. "Nope. They still ain't got shit. We are getting off. Don't worry about it. Everything else is running like clockwork."

We? I ain't going down for this.

I watched a hawk fly over the back of the green fields in front of me, which seemed odd.

"Nicely done. Speak soon." I clicked off the phone. So

that's what she was doing. How dare that bitch try to evade my grasp after all I'd given her? She didn't deserve it. A sinister smile tugged over my lips. Her freedom would be cut short; I just had to be smarter this time. I was a man who knew how to bide his time so I would wait in the shadows, ready to strike.

I called my girl. In my mind she was anyway. My property, and I took care of what I owned.

"Hey baby."

"Hey sexy," she said evenly.

"How you feeling?"

"Good. I'm packing." I felt my heart lurch because I knew our love tryst had come to an end for now.

"I know, let's not start the conversation with that." I cut her short so I could avoid the stark reality of our situation.

"Okay, what do you want to start with, sexy man?"

Her voice was like an eargasm, satin sheets that comforted my dark soul. I didn't deserve her, but I would enjoy her as long as I could.

"Just that I want you to have a beautiful day and that you're a queen. You should have an envelope coming about now." I waited for it. I heard her gasp in delight. "Uh huh. That's how I get down."

"First class flights?"

"That's right. No more economy. At least you can fly back in style. Just remember who put you there."

"Elliot. I can't-" she started to reject it.

"No, you can and you will. It's done. If you need anything, call my private line – you have it. I'm all yours."

"Thank you. I need to tell you something." I felt the tension laced in her voice.

"Tell me baby. What's going on?" I frowned as my stomach knotted a little.

"You need to prepare. You're going to be called back to the States. I'm warning you. I shouldn't. I don't know what the hell I'm doing. You just... I have to get off the phone now, Elliot. Thanks for the flight. Prepare," she said in an exasperated tone. I smiled lightly to myself. Miguel had my back and they had no evidence.

"No chance of that happening," I said with supreme confidence as I heard the front door close and the maid leave.

"Yes, I'm giving you the tip off, new evidence has been found. Get your lawyers together. You're going to need them," she said in her satiny voice. I heard the phone click dead. She hung up on me. Now that air of freedom felt like a stifling wind hitting my face. I turned inside with the inner knowledge that Ms. Clemens cared for me. She just put her ass on the line.

My game was too tight. No matter what, I would continue to reign the chessboard.

20

SARA

♟

"We got him. We got him." I rubbed the sleep out of my eyes. I didn't even know where the hell I was. I was still floating around in a dream state somewhere with Elliot on an expensive yacht in a white bikini.

"What is it that you got, Hawk?" I asked sleepily, the phone hanging lightly against my ear. I continued rubbing my eyes, annoyed that he'd waken me from my last day of slumber in Portugal. I'd planned to sleep in and head into Lisbon. Seemed to be a running theme in my life that I would be interrupted at every turn.

"Forensics has enough on Clope to bring him in," he punched out. I almost choked on my own saliva.

"What the fuck? How? What did they find?" My eyes shot open as I cradled the phone near my ear.

"Clope's hair was found wrapped inside a small piece of rope extracted from the Hudson. The same rope ligature marks matching the rope that Clope brought at the hardware store. They are running another round of DNA tests to confirm. Problem is, I have to keep the intel from Dermas. I don't want him contaminating or tampering with the evidence. He's Team Elliot and we can't afford for that to happen. The case will get thrown out." A heavy lump formed in the middle of my windpipe as I hugged my knees to my chest.

Now, I didn't want Elliot to go to jail. I really didn't. I'd fallen off the cliff of light and plunged into the dark pits of hell along with him. I was wavering. My first instinct was to warn Elliot to prepare. I knew he had money. He had connections, he had enough to beat the case and walk. In my mind I never saw him being convicted, but the voice of Michael Sawyer's father entered my head, challenging my thoughts.

"Whatever it takes. Put him away. I want him to suffer just like Michael did. He blackmailed him. He had no choice."

Evana's frightened face at Elliot's party. "He killed my father, Sara. He killed my father and then married me. The guy is a sick fuck."

I let the salty tears run down my face. My fate was held in this moment. "I hear you. That's good news. He should be convicted," I said gingerly.

"I warned you. I told you not to fall in love with the guy. I knew this was possible. You have to resolve these feelings and move on." Misplaced anger boiled and bubbled as Hawk spoke.

"You don't even know if he will be extradited. He has coverage from the inside here. They won't rat him out. They have money at stake."

Hawk's voice was calm. "He's getting indicted. I received a vision this morning. I'm telling you. I don't know all the details, but my hawk came back from Elliot's villa with a message. It's done. I know you don't want to admit you're in deeper than you think. You let him get to you. I didn't even have time to get in Miguel's ear."

"I didn't. I got you the details. Fixed shipments. You know

everything right down to the last detail. You can't say that." I implied indignantly.

"You have to admit it at least to yourself, Sara. Yes, you did. You got me the intel. Now I'll take it from here because I don't trust your judgement."

I felt my body flush with anger. "Fuck you, Hawk, but thanks for the information. See you in the States."

"Absolutely. Take it easy and I'll take fuck you as a compliment."

I literally could feel Hawk winking through the phone before he clicked off. My heart let me know I was well and truly awake. I sat up and let the sheets fall to the floor.

My moral code was coming into question and staring me in the face. I made my way to the bathroom, washing my face. I looked at myself for more than a few minutes as the water dripped down the sink. *I have to warn Elliot.* This wasn't the imp speaking. It was my heart speaking its truth. We had an ineffable bond, a perfect marriage of light and dark synched together in a typhoon of chaos.

The golden light of the sun's rays warmed the villa, so there was no need to turn on the lights. As I stepped into the villa kitchen to grab a drink, I stopped and recalled part of my conversation to Elliot.

"You need to prepare. You're going to be called back to the States. I'm warning you. I shouldn't. I don't know what the hell I'm doing... You just... I have to get off the phone now Elliot. Thanks for the flight. Prepare."

Some other parts of the conversation I didn't want to think about. I was having an out of body experience talking to Elliot. I clicked off the call quickly, before I regretted my actions and revealed more. A text message came not long after.

You're one of a kind Ms. Clemens. This isn't it for us. Let's focus on what we have.

I'd picked up an envelope that had been slid under my

door with shaky fingers, my breath almost felt like it was going to run out. I opened it, inside was a plane ticket. I looked closer. A first class flight out, for tomorrow, back to New York.

"No more economy. At least you can fly back in style. Just remember who put you there."

"Elliot, I can't-" I couldn't think straight. My head was cloudy as I sipped my drink. I heard my phone beep again. Text messages were flying in from Elliot.

As I picked it up I thought about blocking the number. I would have to discard these messages later. I opened the latest.

Now you just told me where your heart lies. Trust that Sara. Trust us. I'm forever yours. That's not something I would ever declare. Take it as you will. Hold onto it, when it gets rough. Thanks for the heads up.

I STOOD SILENT BREATHING HARD, a bittersweet ending. In the end I did what was right. I sent the manifest through; the shipment would get busted. US Homeland Security knew about it now. This wouldn't be the end though. The whole case was messy and intricately linked with different levels of players across the globe. It would be a battle of the lawyers... would Clope squawk? I doubted it. Would he be protected in prison? How many insiders did Elliot know? Either way the fight was just beginning.

♟

TWO DAYS LATER....

Good to be home. My house had that smell of vacancy. I moved through the rooms touching the walls, checking for abnormalities. Nothing going. I dropped my bag in my room, flopping on my bed. I picked up my phone and switched it from airplane mode. I watched all the calls come in. Hawk. Elliot. Michael Sawyer's father. Shit was getting real. Dermas. Two from him. The café guy. My phone was running hot. I left my room and sat at the kitchen table. I would start with Michael Sawyer's father.

"Hi Sara, nice to hear from you. I assume you heard the news that Clope has been picked up for the murder of my son," he said gruffly.

"Yes. I heard. Good news." I responded flatly, my feelings not telling me which way to feel. "It's not over yet. There's still the trial, and you bet your bottom dollar he will have a strong legal defense; however, the evidence is clear cut. They will need to put some extreme heat on him to make him talk. Clope hails from the old school, and his father was mafia affiliated. There's a street code. No snitching. He upholds that. Plus, we don't know who Elliot has on the inside."

"I know, I'm well aware. But this can lead to Elliot being extradited – then we have a shot. I want Clope to go straight to hell, but I want to cut off the head of the snake and it's the two-bit hustler in a pinstripe suit: Elliot."

"This is confidential and between you and me… His docks are in trouble and he is being watched heavily. No matter what, he will have to go to trial at some stage." At least I could tell him that part.

"ATTA GIRL. I knew I hired the right one. Keep me in the loop. We have to keep breaking Elliot down. Hit him in the pockets where it hurts. Chip away. I want him brought in on tax evasion, company fraud, anything you can think of. Don't let up."

"I'm not in charge of the end result, but we're moving in the right direction."

"Good, good. Speak later, bye Sara."

"Bye."

Time to get back a sense of normalcy, even though nothing would be the same again. I rubbed the back of my head. Only a small ridge existed from my near-death encounter with a mad assassin. Psychologically, I hadn't had a moment to process all the trauma; the hits just kept on rolling. I put on a light jacket. The Jersey air had a little chill to it and I set foot out to the Little Birdy Café for a coffee. I walked in, appreciating the place like never before. I ordered my usual as the Jersey people laughed, young and old; the baristas joked and the coffee machine hissed. Everything was right in the world. The calls came. Dermas. I bit the bullet.

"Hey Dermas. How you doing?"

"I'm great, just wanted to check on you and let you know the news." I played it safe and acted as if I knew nothing.

"What news?" I said as my hot coffee was placed in front of me with a teal mug.

"Clope has been indicted for murder. It's about to be all over the news."

"Wow, so it's happening. That's crazy," I pretended. I think I did a pretty good job.

"Yup. Elliot is being extradited." My stomach turned in knots, I shivered in my chair, this part I didn't know and I hadn't heard from Hawk yet. "Yes. The Portugal authorities have turned him over, he's coming in on a first class flight."

"No handcuffs, right?"

"Nope. He's not seen as a threat somehow. Two Spanish officials will accompany him to the flight, but Elliot is crafty and he got away last time. He might set up a getaway. If he boards the plane, two U.S Marshals in plainclothes will meet and bring him in. Technically, he isn't under arrest. No links have been established between him and Clope. He will be called in as a witness, given Michael Sawyer was directly connected to Elliot through Mescon Technologies."

"I see," I said cautiously. Dermas was trying to make me

comfortable. My mind got to ticking... He might be the one to release Elliot once he landed. My odds were betting on it.

"So I'm guessing you're going to be on ground when Elliot lands?"

"You guessed right. Front and center. We've been waiting on him."

"Uh-huh. Well good luck. By the way, I don't need those prints dusted anymore. I was just being paranoid, I think."

Dermas paused. "You sure? Okay to be careful. I wouldn't want anything happening to you," Dermas said with an undercurrent of warning in his ultra-smooth tone. My body responded by prickles standing up on my neck. Instincts. I sipped my New York coffee. I had to readjust back to it, now I was used to European flavors.

"I'll be fine, and if I need help you will be the first one I call," I said easily.

"Great. I will keep you updated. Prepare for trial, Sara."

"I will for sure." I let the phone die and felt sick, nauseous at the news. Questions filled my mind. Miguel must have turned him in. Elliot's words flashed: *"Trust in us, Sara. Trust in what we have."* I put a hand on my temple. I was sweating. I clenched my fingers and released, trying to get the shake out of them. Didn't work.

"Hello! Earth to Sara." I jumped and looked up.

"Oh hey, Devin, how you doing?" After Robert, Devin looked like a little school boy. I must have been depressed and desperate when I agreed to the date. He was grinning hard. "So how about that date? I'm sorry I didn't call. I had a few things going on, but I'm clear now."

I stared dead in his eyes. "Thanks Devin, but I have a lot to deal with. New cases. I'll see you around." I dropped a twenty on the table and slid past him out of the door and into the Jersey wind. I left him standing with his mouth wide open.

My phone went off. "Dermas."

"I know. He's going to pick him up right? Getaway plan." Hawk was on the line. Great minds think alike.

"No, he won't. I'm going to be on the flight. On the ground. Elliot's not getting away this time. Miguel turned him in. Ratted on him. Big call, since he was set to make millions. But now he has the connections. Smart move on his part. Get ready, Sara."

"I've heard that a lot today" is all I could say. Hawk clicked off the phone as blood rushed through my ears with such force it felt like the torrid current of a raging ocean.

Just like it started. I steadied my hands in the lock of my humble house. I noticed a flash of yellow under the door. This was becoming a habit. I shook it. Bile rose in my throat as I closed my eyes in despair. This couldn't be good news.

I opened it to large high definition photos of Elliot and me kissing, Elliot and me in the hot air balloon, Elliot at my door in the villa, Elliot opening the town car door for me and a note on lined paper.

I know what you did.

I slumped down the door as the slow roll of salty tears dripped to my tiled floor. The irony of it all, the photographs I took for a living to incriminate others turned on me. The pictures in my hands released and scattered to the ground in multiple directions.

THE PAWN; **the weakest in the game. It can never capture the king.** A devil's game taken too far. I was wrapped up in his deceitful arms with a helluva fight to get out.

21

ELLIOT

I sat. I waited in the dark of the villa. A glass of Hennessy easing the ache. Calm. I knew. She told me and that's all that mattered. My first and only love of my life. *Ms. Sara Clemens.* How she managed to love a man like me remained to be seen.

The light to my dark. The sweetness to my bitterness. The caramel to my white-hot chocolate.

Love. Yes, I loved her more than life itself. She'd ripped open my shadowy heart plunging light into it. I knew she'd be back in New York now. I sent the message.

Sara. I love you.

My last message. Then I deleted them all and smashed my phone to smithereens. Clope wouldn't talk. He couldn't. I had too much on him. He would serve life with his track record. Even as the knock came with the boys in blue. Seemed as if the colors were universal. Even as the shock of the double cross from Miguel filtered through my brain.

What a game we played, but you see the King always

wins. He will always retain the throne. I played the long game. Now it was time to show New York what I was really made of...

ABOUT THE AUTHOR

L.R. Starr is both a writer and professional artist residing in down under Australia. She is a lover of twists and turns and the uncovered mysteries of life. Never too far away from nature she can be found planning her next travels or in the realms of her imagination coming up with something creative to keep you inspired and entertained.

You can connect with the author here:

Facebook.com/L.R.STARR1/

INSTAGRAM.COM/L.R.STARR1/

ALSO BY L. R. STARR

If you enjoyed this book highly likely that you would love my Sara Clemens Mystery Series. Check out the heat pounders below.

FireBomb

CheckMate

Book 3 on the way…

www.ingramcontent.com/pod-product-compliance
Lightning Source LLC
Chambersburg PA
CBHW070926250626
47159CB00009B/3142